XTREME MYSTERIES

Lost Wake

#5

Laban Hill

HYPERION PAPERBACKS FOR CHILDREN

NEW YORK

1

"I am the mystery master!" Jamil Smith cried as he spun around the dock. With his beach towel wrapped around his shoulders like a cape, he looked like Sherlock Holmes off on another case. But this time, it was much different. This time Jamil and his X-crew buds—Natalie Whittemore, Kevin Schultz, and Wall Evans—were creating a mystery, not solving one!

His friends laughed as Jamil hammed it up on the edge of the dock at Lake Potow Resort. He moved more like an ox than a giselle.

"I weave the hardest, the craziest, the gnarliest mys . . . whoa . . ." Jamil accidentally stepped on the edge of the dock and lost his balance. "Yiyee!" His left foot caught the heel of his right. "Agh!" His hands grabbed at the air and his arms flailed, but he couldn't right himself.

Splash!

He had grown two inches in the last couple of months and was as thin as a rail. Because of this sudden growth spurt, he wasn't always in control of which way his feet were going.

"Mystery master maybe, but also total feeb," Wall cracked as he watched his friend surface. He was on the opposite side of the dock skipping stones across the glasslike surface of the lake. His arm whipped like a slingshot. The flat stone that he had collected on the shore skimmed across the water, skipping seven times before it disappeared.

Jamil's legs scissored with a snap to keep afloat. "It was the sun's glare," Jamil protested feeling especially sensitive about his awkwardness. "It blinded me."

"Whatever," Nat replied. "I'm the true master. I'm the one who came up with the mystery!" She was mostly right. Of the crew, Nat was the organizer. "It's *my* jewelry that's going to be stolen." She dug into her backpack and fished out the jewelry box that held a fake diamond necklace.

The X-crew had been invited to organize a mystery weekend at the Lake Potow Resort which was owned by a friend of Jamil's dad, Bob Petty. It was a fifty-room hotel nestled in a calm cove of Lake Potow and located just a few miles from Butterbean Ski Slope. In the winter the hotel was always packed. The resort had all kinds of cross-country ski trails and Bob would clear the cove of snow for ice-skating. The resort even sponsored amateur hockey tournaments for guests and locals.

Summer, however, was very slow for the hotel. So this weekend was kind of a trial run for creating more business during the warm months next year.

The kids were totally charged that they had been entrusted with a big part of making sure this weekend was a hit. They were also cranked by the chance to use their mystery-solving skills to stage a mystery of their own.

Nat stood at the edge of the dock looking down at Jamil when a hand came from behind her and gave her a little shove. It was just enough to…*Splash!*…send Nat into Lake Potow. As Nat fell, the jewelry box flew out of her hand high in the air. Wall, the culprit, snagged the box before it fell into the lake. He hopped along the dock's edge to get his balance. "Don't want to lose this." He grinned.

"Good catch," Kevin said. He sat on the edge of the dock dangling his feet in the water. Kevin, the most analytical of the crew, hung back and watched his friends play.

Nat surfaced quickly. She grabbed Wall by the ankles and pulled. Wall tried to recover his balance but was already falling forward. He spun toward Kevin and tossed him the jewelry box and then…*Splash!*

Wall surfaced. "Hey, Kev," he shouted to Kevin, the only one of the four still on the dock. "Could you give me hand?" Wall reached up toward the dock.

Kevin scooted away from the edge and stood quickly. "No way. I'm not coming over there." Alone on the dock he stood with his legs apart like the king of the hill. His dark brown skin and close-cropped afro stood out against the sun-bleached wood planks of the dock. "Besides, I've got to hang onto the loot." He waved the jewelry box at his friend.

"You got me wrong," Wall replied, trying not to smile. "I'm not going to pull you in. I just need some help getting out of the water."

Kevin held his ground. "Use the ladder."

"Chicken!" Jamil taunted.

"You got that right," Kevin answered.

Nat swam over to the ladder and climbed onto the dock. Her long blond hair spread out like a fan on her bare back.

Kevin grabbed his towel and rolled it into a rat tail. Then he dipped the tip in the water.

Snap!

"You're dead meat if that touches me," Nat warned as she pointed at Kevin. "Don't even think about it." She grabbed her towel and quickly rolled it into a rat tail.

"Truce," Kevin said when he saw Nat ready to do battle. He let his towel harmlessly unravel.

Wall disappeared underwater, swam under the dock, and surfaced behind Nat. He reached up to grab her ankle, but she saw him out of the corner of her eye.

"Too slow!" Nat shouted as she danced across the dock.

Suddenly, the growl of a motorboat's engine filled the air. A few seconds later, the boat came into view from around the edge of the cove. It was a big white motorboat that churned up a monster wake. Behind it a sleek,

4

tanned man wakeboarded. He shot fakie across the wide wake of the boat. Then he cut back and uncoiled high in the air. As he sailed above both wakes and spun a 180, he seemed to take all the time in the world. It felt like an hour before he landed outside the opposite wake.

"Perfect half-cab!" Jamil gasped in total awe. "I was close to doing that last summer." The previous summer Jamil and his family had vacationed with cousins in Minnesota. He had spent two glorious weeks wakeboarding every day.

"That must be Kyle Rodriguez," Kevin said. "Wasn't he last year's tour champ?" Kyle Rodriguez was scheduled to perform an exhibition this weekend at the resort.

The boarder let go of the handle. As he held his hand up like he was riding a wild bronco, he sprung a lightning-fast tantrum.

"Doesn't he get dizzy?" Nat asked after the rider had landed his back flip.

"He rules!" Kevin shouted as he pumped his fist in the air. "I got to learn how to do that."

To catch a better view, Wall pulled himself up on the dock and whipped his long brown hair behind him, sending a spray of water into the air.

The motorboat cut a double up that sent the rollers off to the side away from the boat's wake. This made the lake's surface perfect for a second pass—no chop.

"That boat must have a massive water bag. Look at the wake!" Wall said with admiration. Wall was hard-wired for all kinds of obscure facts. Like the heavier the load in the boat, the bigger the wake. And one great way to increase the load was to add bags full of water, sand, or concrete.

Out on the water, the wakeboarder caught a radical edge and shot like a bullet back across the wake. This time he took a wide progressive backside approach and kicked his board directly over his head for another gnarly tantrum. But instead of whipping through the trick, this time his board hovered over his head before he rolled his shoulders upward and landed outside the boat's wake. It was like watching him in slo-mo replay on TV.

"Awesome hang time!" Jamil said. "I can only do a surface three-sixty and a two wake one-eighty."

"We've got to make sure we spend major wake time this weekend," Nat exclaimed.

"Hold on, you guys," Kevin cut in as he watched his friends get distracted by the wakeboarder. "Before we learn to ride, we've got to make sure we're ready for the mystery."

Earlier in the summer Jamil's dad, Ned Smith, had bragged at a regional resort hotel conference about Jamil and his friends' ability to solve mysteries. Mr. Smith ran Hoke Valley Ski Resort. Bob Petty had overheard Mr. Smith, and asked him if the crew would be interested in staging a mystery at his hotel.

When the crew learned about the offer, they went nuts. Not only because of the job, but also because they were doing the mystery for a big wakeboarding weekend sponsored by Wake Ever Boards, one of the hottest manufacturers around. What made it even better was the fact that Kyle Rodriguez, wakeboarding's twenty-six-year-old golden boy, would be there.

The motorboat's engine throttled down to a low growl as it slowed to pick up the wakeboarder. When the boat came alongside the dock, Jamil grabbed the line tossed to him from the boat. He secured it with a quick figure-eight knot. "Gnarly ride!"

"Thanks," said the guy as he jumped onto the dock. "I'm Kyle." He must have been at least a foot taller than any of them.

"We know," Kevin replied. "We've seen you on TV."

Wall jumped into the boat to examine the water bag in the rear. "What's this weigh? Six hundred pounds?" Wall asked the woman driving.

The woman turned around and smiled. "Exactly six hundred. Good guess."

Wall patted the bag. "Well, not really a guess. I saw one like this in a wakeboarding catalog."

"You ride?" she asked.

"Well…" Wall hesitated. He wanted to lie and say he did, but he knew he'd be busted. "Not yet. But I want to learn."

"It's so cool you're here this weekend," Jamil said to Kyle. "We're the ones staging the mystery weekend."

"Awesome!" Kyle grinned and turned toward the boat's driver. "Hey, April, come meet these dudes."

April climbed out of the boat. "I'm April Winston, World Wakeboarding Association's tour manager." From the size of her arms and shoulders, the crew could tell she spent a lot of time wakeboarding, too. She was tanned and her hair was sun-bleached just like Kyle's. She shook everyone's hands as they introduced themselves.

Kyle reached into the boat and grabbed his wakeboarding bag. It was so packed with equipment that it couldn't be zipped closed. He dropped it on the dock, and half the stuff spilled out.

As Jamil looked down and admired Kyles collection of gloves and flotation vests, he noticed a white enveloped stuffed with papers that were falling out. "You're going to lose that stuff." He pointed to the envelope.

Kyle bent over and stuffed the papers back inside. "Thanks."

Kevin noticed the return address on the envelope. It read SPLASH BOARDS. "I thought you were riding for Wake Ever Boards," Kevin commented with confusion as he pointed at the envelope.

Kyle froze. "Uh … well … I am." He quickly buried the envelope in his bag. "That's why I'm here this weekend. Wake Ever is the weekend's sponsor." He stood and waved dismissively toward his bag. "Those are just some catalogs. I can look at their stuff. I just can't use it."

April snorted. Nat noticed her giving Kyle a cold look.

There was suddenly an awkward silence. It was broken when April changed the subject. "You want to ride?" she asked the gang. "We've still got half a tank of gas." She started to climb back in the boat.

"Yes!" Wall said without thinking. He was totally stoked.

Jamil wanted to ride, too, but he kept quiet and stepped away from the boat. A whole year had passed by since he last rode. Besides, his growth spurt hadn't helped his confidence any. And Jamil always felt like he had to try harder because he was twelve, a whole year younger than his friends.

Then he remembered that they were meeting with the actors in the mystery in about twenty minutes. A wave of relief washed over him. He had a real reason not to board right now. "Can we do it later?"

"Sure," Kyle answered. "We're not going anywhere."

"We still have to set up some stuff," Nat explained. She glanced up at the three-story hotel. It sat about two hundred yards up a grassy, gentle slope, nestled among tall pines. The planning meeting with the actors was going to be on the porch that overlooked Lake Potow.

Wall turned to his friends and bounced excitedly on the balls of his feet. "Do you need me? It sounds like things are in pretty good shape."

Jamil shrugged. "I think Nat and I can take care of it. But I want you to be ready for tomorrow." He squeezed the water out of his wet towel. "Why don't you hang, too, Kev?"

Kevin smiled. "Excellent. I was hoping you'd say that. I'm stoked for a deep water start." Both Kevin and Wall hopped into the boat. April cranked up the engine.

"You guys ever ride before?" Kyle asked.

They shook their heads.

"Don't worry. It's a snap," Kyle replied. "Just do what I say."

"I think there's a board with straps in that shed," April said as she pointed to a small building where the dock met the shore.

"I'd let you use mine, but I've got high wraps and they're sized to my feet," said Kyle. He turned and ran up the dock. He disappeared into the shed for a second and came out with a wakeboard. "It's directional, but that shouldn't matter if you're just learning." He held up a wakeboard that looked more like a surfboard with a fin only on the tail. This style was pretty outdated. Manufacturers had come up with a twin-style design. Wakeboards now looked like half-pipe snowboards with fins on both ends. Kyle ran back down the dock.

"All I want is to ride some wakes." Wall grinned.

"Then, let's rock," Kyle replied as he hopped in the motor boat.

April revved up the engine and backed away from the dock.

"Knock yourselves out," Nat called as she waved to her friends. She and Jamil then started up the dock to the shore.

On the slope leading to the hotel, Jamil noticed that the place needed a good scrape and paint job. This suprised him a little since upkeep at his dad's resort was his dad's obssession. He knew his dad would never have let their place look so bad.

"Do you think Kyle was telling the truth?" Nat asked.

"About what?" Jamil asked.

"About what's in that envelope," Nat explained. "I mean, those weren't catalogs. There were letters in there."

"That's weird," Jamil replied. "Why would he lie about some letters?"

"Maybe he's thinking of jumping sponsors," Nat suggested.

Jamil stopped in his tracks. "That would be totally bent—coming up here for Wake Ever this weekend and then jumping to Splash Boards."

"Rude," Nat agreed.

Nat and Jamil turned on the bottom step leading to porch as they heard the boat's engine rev. The day was perfect for being out on the water—cloudless and windless.

About seventy feet behind the boat, they watched Kevin slowly rise out of a deep water start. Once up, he pitched immediately onto his face.

"Dank! That's way stylin'!" Nat shouted as she watched Kevin go down.

She and Jamil turned back toward the hotel. Coming down the broad steps was a guy wearing Day-Glo orange wrap-around shades and sporting a trimmed goatee. He carried a large green board bag slung over his shoulder. He nodded to Nat and Jamil. "Here for the mystery weekend?"

"Yes, we're the organizers. You're early," Jamil commented. "I thought guests weren't arriving until later this afternoon."

"I wanted to get some riding in before there was a line," he replied. "That is if I can get their attention." He looked out at the motorboat roaring across the lake. Then he turned back to Nat and Jamil. "I'm Evan," he said, like he expected them to already know that.

Jamil held out his hand and introduced Nat and himself.

Evan's eyes wandered toward the lake as he shook Jamil's hand. Jamil and Nat felt like he wasn't really interested in them.

"You like to ride?" Jamil asked. Of the crew, he was the best at getting people to talk. He was a natural at it. This time, however, he didn't expect much success.

"Wakeboarding is life," Evan answered. "If I could afford it, I'd ride year-round. But some people just aren't as lucky as good old Kyle."

Nat and Jamil looked each other. What sort of beef could this guy have with Kyle?

"I'd miss snowboarding," Jamil said. "But I know what you mean. I'd rather be riding than doing anything else."

Nat looked at her watch. "We've got to go. See you, Evan."

"Later," Evan replied as he headed toward the dock. A pair of teal wakeboarding gloves hung out of his back pocket.

When Evan was out of range to hear her, Nat commented, "That guy must spend a couple of hours in front of the mirror every morning."

"He is fully accessorized," Jamil smirked. "I wonder if he can ride at all? Sounds like he's just a bit jealous of Kyle."

"Whether he is or not," Nat replied, "I hope he stays down there for a while. I don't want him seeing us meeting with the actors." They watched Evan dump his bag on the dock and unzip it. He pulled out the most expensive Wake Ever wakeboard out of his bag. Then he laid two totally stylin' life vests, his own towrope, and several other things beside it on the dock.

"I don't think we'll have to worry about him," Jamil replied. "He's probably too wrapped up in taking care of his stuff to even participate in the mystery." They headed into the hotel. "Let's find Bob and get this meeting going before anyone else arrives."

"Yeah," Nat agreed.

As Jamil and Nat crossed the threshold of the lobby, the smell of mildew tickled his nose. Again, he was surprised. His dad worked so hard to keep the carpets at Hoke Valley really clean to prevent mildew. He knew from his dad's complaints that the job was nearly impossible. Jamil would have assumed Bob Petty was just as concerned about it. But Bob wasn't.

This made Jamil look at the interior of the hotel more closely. The lobby looked old. It was very rustic, with antelope horns, stuffed trout, and nature prints lining the walls. Not a surprise up in the mountains. And the center of the room was dominated by a large, circular fireplace that would be heaven in the winter. But what struck Jamil was that everything had a thin film of dust over it. The antlers housed a couple of cobwebs and the fireplace looked like it hadn't been cleaned out since March. Even though Jamil was a total slob, he knew this was not the way to run a hotel.

Bob Petty was standing behind the redwood front desk talking to Jamil's dad, Ned Smith. Mr. Smith had driven the gang up for the mystery weekend and planned to enjoy a few days at the resort. He was looking forward to not having anything to do.

"Nat! Jamil! Perfect timing," Bob said as he waved them over. "Let's have that meeting." He was full of bubbly, infectious energy.

"Great," Jamil replied as he leaned against the desk.

"I'll ring up the actors and have them meet us on the porch," Bob said as he grabbed the phone. "It's a perfect day to be outside." After he called the actors, he looked out into the lobby. "Wimple!"

"Y-yes, sir?" a frail, reedy voice called from across the lobby. An old man with hardly any meat on his bones came toward them. His uniform hung on him like it was on a hanger.

Jamil and Nat hadn't noticed Wimple when the came in. They watched him make his way slowly across the lobby.

"Would you please set up some chairs at the far end of the porch?" Bob asked him.

Wimple nodded and shuffled outside.

"Do you think he can handle it?" Nat whispered to Jamil.

"Maybe we should help him," Jamil replied. He was a little worried that Wimple might have a heart attack lifting one of the chairs. "But first I want to know if Wimple is his first name or last."

They both laughed.

"I'll catch you guys at supper," Mr. Smith said as he retreated down the hall to his room. "I'm going to catch some shut-eye. I can't remember the last time I took a nap during the day."

"Knock yourself out, Dad," Jamil called after him.

"Remember 'The good are those who perform their trust and fail not in their word, and keep their pledge,'" said Mr. Smith to Jamil and Nat.

"Right, Dad. Thanks for the advice," Jamil replied. He was used to his dad talking like that, but he never really understood what he meant.

"Your dad is *so* weird," Nat said. "My parents like to tell me what to do, but your dad totally beats them when it comes to parental advice. All they ever say is, 'you'll poke an eye out' or something like that. Your dad talks like some sort of sensei."

"Yeah, I know." Jamil sighed. "He's still stuck on those crazy sayings he learned when he and my mom went through a Sikh religious phase about fifteen years ago. That's why I'm named Jamil and not Mike or Ed."

A few minutes later, an odd assortment of people joined Nat, Jamil, and Bob on the porch. First a woman bounded onto the porch. She flashed them a one hundred watt, leading-lady smile and strode to where they had gathered a few chairs. Behind her came a round, bespectacled older gentleman whose neatly trimmed gray beard and pressed white summer suit suggested a person of great elegance and culture. He was followed by a guy in his early twenties wearing a wet suit and carrying a wakeboard. But it was the last person to come through the door that completely floored Nat and Jamil.

This guy was huge! He had to walk through the doorway sideways because his shoulders couldn't fit the normal way. His arms were as big as Jamil's and Nat's thighs put together.

"He could probably lift this building," Jamil whispered to Nat.

"At least," Nat gasped.

Bob bounced to his feet and smiled. "These are our actors for the weekend." He turned to the woman. "This is Naomi Pleasants." He nodded to the older gentleman. "This is Ralph Cousins. He's actually my brother-in-law. He's done a lot of acting in England."

Mr. Cousins bowed. "Pleased to meet you."

"I'm Nick Adams," the wakeboarder added as he reached out to shake Nat's and Jamil's hands.

Bob turned to shoulders. "And this is Mr. Lars Pupchick."

"Delighted," Mr. Pupchick said in a vaguely European accent.

Everyone sat down and got right to business.

Jamil first pointd to Mr. Pupchick. "You're the villain, as you know." He flipped through the pages of the script

17

while Nat handed copies to everyone. "You'll be the bell captain and the thief. Your two different-sized feet are really coming in handy. Did you bring the leather shoes we asked you to?"

"I have them right here," Mr. Pupchick answered, pulling out a pair of black leather shoes with thick rubber soles. "One's a size ten and the other is an eleven."

Jamil smiled. This was going better than he had expected. "And you guys are also a size ten?"

Nick and Mr. Cousins both nodded.

"All right." Jamil glanced at the script. "That will set up the red herrings and give the guests their major clue. I'll need the shoes later tonight, Mr. Pupchick, so I can plant them. But I want to make sure the guests see you in them. Then, hopefully, they'll notice tomorrow when you're wearing the black sneakers instead."

"Sounds fine," replied Mr. Pupchick. "And please, call me Lars."

Jamil turned to Naomi Pleasants. "Ms. Pleasants, you're obviously the victim."

She smiled. "Naomi, please." She pulled her large mane of curly black hair into a bun on top of her head.

"Here's the jewelry," Nat said as she handed the box to Naomi.

Naomi opened the box and held the jeweled necklace up to the light. "It looks almost real."

"Real enough for this," Nat said. "Be careful with it. It's my mom's."

"Sure thing, hon," Naomi said as she popped a stick

of gum in her mouth.

Nat winced. "And one more thing. Could you make sure you don't act completely helpless? The whole damsel in distress thing is so cliché. I don't want our mystery to be like that. Try getting angry instead of hysterical and all upset."

"Whatever you say," Naomi replied with a crack of her gum.

"I just wish a guy was the victim," Nat muttered.

"We already discussed this," Jamil said impatiently. "You agreed that the necklace was the best prop. And the only person who would have the necklace would be a woman."

"I know, but I just don't want her to act like some helpless ditz," Nat said defensively.

"Noted." Jamil then turned to Mr. Cousins. "You're Naomi's guardian."

Mr. Cousins nodded. "Righto, old chap," he answered in his British accent.

Nat smiled. "The accent's a nice addition to the role."

"And, Nick," continued Jamil, "you're the international jewel thief who has given up your life of crime.

"I've always wanted to be a jewel thief," Nick replied as he sat up straight.

"*Reformed* jewel thief," Nat emphasized. "Remember, you're not the thief. Any question?" Everyone shook their heads. "Then let's go through the script."

After about an hour, Jamil wrapped up the meeting. "Don't forget that only the details of the mystery and your background must be stuck to. You can improvise your dialogue."

The actors nodded.

Then Jamil turned to Lars. "I'll need those shoes before you go to bed. I want to plant one under Naomi's window tonight. But I want the guests to see you wearing them tonight. The other has to turn up later on." Jamil absentmindedly picked at the seat cushion of his chair. It had a small tear in it and he had worried out a tiny bit of the stuffing.

"Bob, how soon will guests be arriving?" Nat asked.

The sound of tires crunching on the gravel driveway answered Nat's question.

"I guess we better break this up before someone sees us," Jamil said.

Bob stood and looked at Nat and Jamil. "I sure hope nothing goes wrong. I've got too much riding on the success of this weekend." Bob half smiled, but the worried look on his face didn't disappear. "I'm depending on you guys to live up to your reputations."

Everyone stood to leave, except Jamil. He suddenly felt like a thousand pounds had been dropped on his shoulders. Bob might have just jinxed the whole weekend. How could something not go wrong, now that he's brought it up? Jamil wasn't superstitious, but he would have preferred never having the possibility of trouble even mentioned.

Rubber chicken.

That's what Jamil's dad called chicken that was over-cooked and tough to chew. He said bad chicken was a sign of a bad hotel. Jamil couldn't tell the difference between a rubber chicken and a perfectly cooked one, but he figured that if any place was going to serve it, it would be this place. Everything else here was pretty shabby, why would the chicken be an exception?

Jamil spotted his dad and friends at a table to one side of the dining room. "Everybody ready?" Jamil asked, walking up to them.

"This mystery is going to be so cool," Wall replied.

Jamil glanced around the room. There were about twenty-five guests, seated at four other tables. He spotted Naomi and Mr. Cousins at one table. Nick sat at another with a bunch of totally rad wakeboarders. Naomi was fiddling very conspicuously with the "diamond"

necklace around her neck. Jamil smiled. She was doing her job.

"Where's Lars?" Jamil asked. "He's got to make himself visible."

"Don't worry," Nat replied. "He's right over there." She pointed to Lars standing by the doors to the kitchen. The shoulders of his white waiter's jacket looked like a shelf large enough to stack dishes on.

"Do you think he should do something?" Jamil asked. "I'm just afraid that no one will suspect him as the perp since he supposedly works for the hotel."

"Shhh! Not so loud," Kevin cautioned. He glanced at the nearby tables to see if anyone overheard them. He saw Evan at the next table looking at them with a curious expression.

Jamil apologized. "But don't you think he should have a higher profile?"

"Yeah, you don't want him to disappear into the paneling like Wimple," Nat cracked.

"How about we get Lars to spill a tray of plates or something," Wall suggested.

"You guys are a trip," Mr. Smith commented. "I'm going to get something to drink while you finish scheming." He got up and headed over to the bar.

"Hey, wait!" Jamil called after him. "Could you get me a Coke?" Then he turned to his friends. "What do you guys want?"

"What am I a waiter?" Mr. Smith cracked. "'No father has given his child anything better than good manners.'"

Jamil buried his head in his hands. "Not another saying. I always know when I've done wrong when he starts with the sayings," Jamil protested jokingly.

Everyone laughed.

"It's all right. What do you kids want?" Mr. Smith looked at Nat, Wall, and Kevin.

They all gave him their orders and knew to say please when they did.

"Back to Lars," Jamil said as his dad left.

The crew leaned into the table and began whispering. After a minute they all settled back in their chairs with smiles of satisfaction. Jamil got up and disappeared into the kitchen looking for Bob.

He returned about five minutes later. "It's taken care of," he told his friends.

"What is?" Mr. Smith asked as he passed the sodas around the table.

"You'll see, Dad," Jamil replied.

His friends smiled conspiratorially as he said this.

At that moment, Bob came through the kitchen doors and motioned to Lars to come in the kitchen. A few seconds later, Bob came back out with a large tray filled with plates. Behind him came Wimple and Lars, each with a tray of food as well.

"This should be good," Mr. Smith said as he watched them spread out across the room.

"Really?" Jamil asked with surprise.

"Are you kidding? Maggie, Bob's wife, is a four-star chef," Mr. Smith replied. "That's why this place is so booked in the winter. The food is incredible." He shook his napkin and spread it out on his lap.

Lars came to their table and winked as he set beautifully decorated plates on the table. "Tonight's dinner is rainbow trout with a strawberry and jalepeño puree."

Jamil looked nervously down at his plate. Maybe rubber chicken wasn't so bad after all. "After seeing the lobby, I was a little worried."

"Don't worry. Bob runs a great hotel. He's just usually not open in the summer, so the place isn't in perfect condition," Mr. Smith explained.

Jamil nodded.

"Bob's taking a huge gamble in trying establish a summer business. It would be a big help if the Professional Wakeboarding Tour decided to stage a competition here next year. This weekend is kind of a test run." Mr. Smith took a bite of the trout. "Hmmm! This is delicious."

The crew looked at him nervously. They weren't sure about the food. They were more used to hot dogs and fries than they were strawberry and jalapeño puree.

"The potatoes are good," Nat said without much enthusiasm.

Jamil pushed the fish to the opposite side of the plate from the puree. "Does this have bones?"

"Yes," Mr. Smith replied. "But the trout is so fresh is melts like butter in your mouth."

"This *is* good," Wall said with some surprise as he took a miniscule bite of the trout.

"All right, I'll try it," Kevin said. He took a bite. He

was also surprised to discover he liked the fish. "Try it, you'll like it," he said to Nat and Jamil.

After their initial reluctance, the crew enjoyed their dinner in silence. This was always a sign that the food was good. Everyone was concentrating on eating.

Bob entered the dining room with a triangle and clanged it lightly. "Attention! Attention, everyone! I want to welcome you all to the Wake Ever Mystery Weekend."

Applause erupted around the room.

"I want to introduce to you the people behind this weekend," Bob continued. "First, there's Joe Yardley, founder and president of Wake Ever. Stand up, Joe."

More applause.

"And Dave Resnick, the creative genius behind Wake Ever's cutting-edge technology."

Mr. Resnick stood quickly and nodded.

"Next, there's April Winston. She's the event director for the Professional Wakeboarding Tour, and she's responsible for deciding if Lake Potow will be the site of next year's Wake Ever Masters Championship."

April rose to applause.

"Finally," Bob paused dramatically. "Here is someone that I'm sure you're all familiar with. Kyle Rodriguez, last year's number one wakeboarder and, so far this season, the tour's top rider."

Kyle stood quickly and nodded to the guests.

When the applause died down, Bob turned to the crew. "Now, I'd like to introduce the people who will be your mystery hosts for the weekend." He waved his hand toward the crew's table. "Jamil Smith, Nat Whittemore, Kevin Schultz, and Wall Evans. Jamil, why don't you take over."

Jamil stood and looked at the crowd nervously. The only time he'd ever spoken to a large group was in school. And that didn't really count because he knew the kids there. "Um. Welcome to Lake Potow's Mystery Weekend. If you don't already know, the thief, along with a few red herrings, are scattered among you. But you might not know right away who he or she is, so think of everyone as a suspect."

People in the audience nodded.

"Wall, could you hand out the weekend's itinerary?" Jamil asked.

Wall stood and handed out a sheet of paper.

Lake Potow Mystery Weekend Itinerary

Friday Evening
9:00 P.M. Evening of great music with the Debbies. Get to know the others at Lake Potow. One might just be the thief!

Saturday
8:00 A.M. Breakfast. You never know when evil will strike. Remember: all guests are suspects. Beware!

10:30 A.M. Wakeboarding exhibition by Kyle Rodriguez.

12:00 P.M. Lunch

2:00 P.M. Wakeboarding Skills Clinic. Kyle Rodriguez and Wake Ever offer tips and tricks to guests.

6:30 P.M. Hors d'oeuvres in the lobby. Slueths hand in solutions.

8:00 P.M. Dinner

9:30 P.M. The crime is solved. Prizes are awarded.

Sunday
9:00 A.M. Breakfast
11:00 A.M. Check out

"As you can see, tomorrow is sprinkled with investigation and wakeboarding. The deadline for submitting your solutions to the crime is six-thirty. Enjoy the weekend."

Bob stood again. "Thanks, Jamil. Now dessert will be served, and afterward the music will begin on the porch."

Lars and Wimple came through the kitchen doors with trays of desserts. Right by the door, Lars seemed to trip. His tray crashed to the floor. Fruit tarts splattered all over the floor.

Everyone's attention was drawn to Lars.

"Don't worry! We still have enough dessert," Lars said loudly as he began picking up the mess.

"Ouch!" Kevin said. "Bob was cool with this?"

"Don't worry," Jamil replied. "There are plenty of desserts. And the plates are old, chipped ones. It was Bob's idea."

"Very sneaky," Nat said with glee. "Nobody could

have overlooked Lars now."

From the porch, strains of some really awesome chords drifted in to the dining room.

"The band's warming up!" Wall said excitedly.

Mr. Smith smiled. "Bob said you'll really like them. He wants you guys to have some fun this weekend."

Jamil, Nat, Kevin, and Wall bolted from their seats without finishing their desserts. On the porch two women were tuning up their guitars while another warmed up at the drums. The crew settled on the lawn right in front of them. As they waited for the concert to begin, the other guests wandered out.

Jamil noticed Evan talking to the Wake Ever people as they came out. He nudged Wall. "What do you want to bet that Evan guy is trying to get them to sponsor him?"

"Why do you say that?" Wall asked. "Who is he?"

"He's some total loser Nat and I met on the way into the hotel while you and Kevin were wakeboarding," Jamil replied. "He's all style and no substance. He has all the latest equipment. But talking to him, you start to wonder if he can really perform on the board. Besides, he's got some weird thing about Kyle. Almost sounded like he was a little jealous that Kyle gets to do the thing he loves best—wakeboarding."

"Yeah," Nat agreed. "That dude would just love to take Kyle's place."

"What a leech," Wall cracked.

"Well, you have to admit. It's a great way to get good

swag," Kevin commented. He hunched his shoulders as he wrapped his arms around his knees. It was getting cool and he hadn't worn a long-sleeve shirt.

"Like you need it," said Jamil. Like Nat and Wall, Jamil envied Kevin's luck. His parents owned a sporting goods store. Kevin never lacked for the most radical equipment.

The crew settled back and listened to the concert.

The lead singer, dressed in a jumpsuit that looked like alligator skin, strummed her electric guitar. "Ladies and gentlemen, thanks for inviting us tonight. We're The Debbies."

The crowd applauded politely.

"Our first song is called 'Wipe It,'" she said. Then she stepped back from the mike and lit into it. The Debbies were a really fresh garage surf band. Their riffs rocked out and the audience grooved.

The Debbies' set lasted about forty-five minutes. Afterward the guests mingled on the porch.

"Let's make sure our actors are seeding the mystery," Jamil suggested. The crew strolled from group to group to listen in on conversations.

"Yes, I'm an heiress, and Mr. Cousins is my guardian," Naomi was telling about half the guests. "At least, until I turn twenty-one and take control of my trust fund myself." The tips of her fingers danced across the jewels of the necklace.

A few feet away, Mr. Cousins was sitting with five guests. "I'm responsible for Naomi. At least for the next two years." He sighed. "Then who knows?"

By the steps Nick spoke to a couple of guests about traveling around the world to wakeboard. As he spoke, he rubbed the diamond tattoo on his hand.

Lars made his rounds with a tray of drinks for the guests. He made sure that he spoke at least a word or two with each guest so that they had to look directly at him.

"Things are going pretty well," Nat said. "Let's go for a walk." The crew headed for the pebble beach. The night sky was virtually cloudless. A light breeze came off the lake.

"You could read a book out here," Jamil said as he looked up at the bright stars.

"Hey, there's Cassiopeia," Kevin said as he pointed to a group of stars. "My dad says…"

"I'm sick of it and I'm sick of you!" a woman's voice came across the lake as if the person was standing right next to them.

"Wait! Wait!" another voice called. This was a man's voice.

Then there was a crash through the woods.

"Duck! They're coming this way," Wall said. The crew hid behind a beach rowboat just as April appeared out of the trees at the opposite end of the clearing. She kicked some rocks and turned toward the hotel.

"April!" Kyle suddenly appeared. He was running after April. "Why do you care? It's just a business decision."

"Uh-oh. Trouble in paradise," Nat cracked.

Necrason rides the waves!

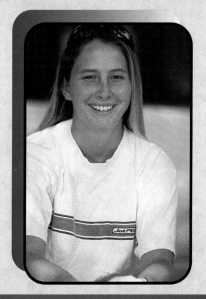

Wakeboarder Jaime Necrason

When Jaime Necrason first saw her brother wake-boarding in 1996, she thought to herself, this looks easy. But as soon as she got on a wakeboard, she realized that the sport was much harder than it looked! After training with pros like Tina Bessinger, Jaime soon began competing in early 1997.

At the Orlando stop of the Pro Tour, Jaime qualified third out of 13 girls. This placement qualified her as a pro on the Pro Tour as well as for ESPN's X Games. Since then she has competed in major competitions on the Pro Tour, and has been featured in such publications as *Wakeboarding, Seventeen, Launch, W,* and *USA Today*. She has also been invited to compete in the U.S. Masters, one of the most prestigious water-ski tournaments in the U.S.

Jaime lives in Winter Park, Florida. She plans to enter college in the fall of 2000 to pursue a degree in veterinary medicine.

BACKROLL

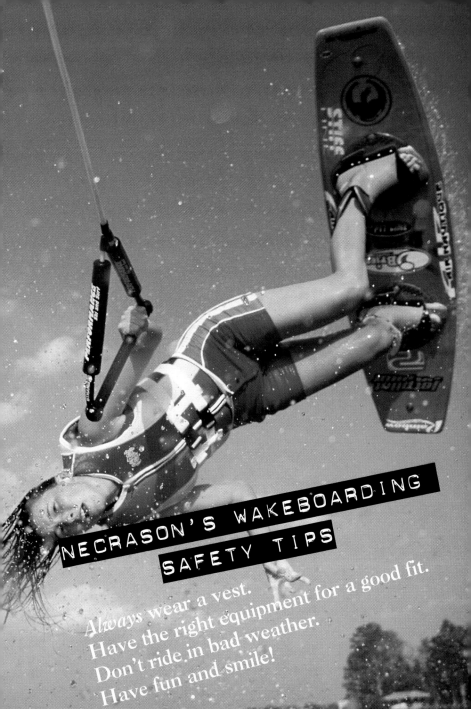

NECRASON'S WAKEBOARDING
SAFETY TIPS

Always wear a vest.
Have the right equipment for a good fit.
Don't ride in bad weather.
Have fun and smile!

Jaime at age 7

Age: 16

Most memorable competition: The ESPN X Games. It was the biggest and most prestigious tournament I have been to yet!

Favorite athlete: Lisa Anderson, because she has done so much for women in surfing. I hope to do the same for wakeboarding.

Favorite wakeboard: My O'brien Heretic board, behind my Air Nautique Boat.

What I like best about my sport: The fact that you can go out with a group of friends and just have fun. That's what it's all about!

Favorite thing to do on a Saturday: Sleep in!

Favorite pig-out food: Fruit roll-ups

Favorite movie: *The Lion King*

"No kidding. Do you think it has anything to do with that envelope from Splash Boards this afternoon?" Jamil asked.

Kevin stood and watched April and Kyle disappear into the hotel. "If it doesn't, then my name is Mickey Mouse."

"Okay, Mickey," Wall replied. "Let's get some sleep. Tomorrow's going to be a long day."

4

The annoying sound of crickets echoed across the lake. A frog's ribbit and then splash accented the hum of crickets rubbing their legs. This was interupted by the sharp buzzing of a mosquito.

Smack! Jamil smushed the fat mosquito on his hand. A bubble of blood smeared across his knuckles. Jamil sat impatiently on the porch of the hotel waiting for Lars. He was supposed to meet him at half past midnight. It was already one in the morning. The entire hotel was quiet except for the insistent sounds of tireless bugs. Normally, Jamil didn't mind crickets, but he was tired and they reminded him of the whine of his history teacher's lecture. She just went on and on...

Creak!

Jamil nearly jumped out of his skin. He turned and saw Lars stepping onto the porch. "You almost gave me a heart attack."

Lars apologized.

"What took you so long?" Jamil whispered.

"I fell asleep," Lars replied.

"That's what I wish I was doing," Jamil said. "I guess I should have just let you drop them off in my room."

"Next time," Lars said as he handed Jamil a pair of black leather shoes with thick rubber soles. He yawned and turned to go back to bed.

Jamil tiptoed down the steps of the porch and flicked on his flashlight. He made his way around the side of the building. He slipped off his sandals and put on Lars's shoes. It was like wearing clown shoes. He hurried over to Naomi's window and then stomped away toward the woods. After about ten feet he let one shoe slip off. Then he limped back to the porch where he put back on his sandals.

The low growl of the motorboat echoed across the lake as it idled just outside the cove. Jamil sat on the side of the boat and slipped into the cold, early morning water. The sun sat low on the eastern edge of the lake.

Jamil's life vest cut into his underarms as he tread water. His dad slid the wakeboard down to him.

"Now, remember how you did it last year," Mr. Smith said gently. "You're probably a little rusty, so don't be surprised if you can't do everything right away."

Jamil nodded and ran through in his mind exactly what he had to do to get up on the board. As Jamil strapped his feet in, he was more worried about his clumsiness getting in the way of his riding than being rusty. He was glad his dad had agreed to come out here to practice while everyone else was still eating breakfast. If he couldn't get up on the board, he would definitely feel major embarrassment. He didn't want that to happen in front of an audience.

Mr. Smith tossed Jamil the rope and put the boat in gear. The rope uncoiled as the boat moved away from Jamil. When it was straight, Mr. Smith threw the boat back into idle. Jamil floated on his back with the board parallel to the water. He gave his dad the thumbs-up sign. Again his dad threw the boat into gear. Slowly the rope went taut, and Jamil began to move forward. Pressure on the board pushed his knees into his chest. He pulled his arms in so that his elbows touched his stomach. He signaled his dad one more time.

Like a monster waking from sleep, the boat's engine roared. The rope jerked Jamil hard. He felt like his arms were being pulled out of their sockets. His muscles clenched and he tucked his elbows back into his belly. His chin slipped below the neck of his vest and his teeth ground tightly. As the boat picked up speed, the wakeboard lifted Jamil out of the water. Jamil fought to keep his body crouched and his arms tucked. He leaned back on the board and pushed it forward. The seat of his swimsuit skimmed along the water's surface. The water stabilized below the board. Jamil was now out of the water. He breathed a sigh of relief and straightened his legs.

"Whoa!" Jamil cried as he flipped face-forward into

the water. It was like hitting pavement. He swallowed a mouthful of water. The rope jerked out of his hands and he rolled onto his back coughing.

Mr. Smith threw the boat into low and circled back to Jamil. "You stood up too fast," he shouted.

Jamil grabbed the rope as it slipped by him. He wasn't particularly receptive to his dad's coaching.

"Riches are not from abundance of worldly skills, but from a contented mind," Mr. Smith cautioned his son.

"Enough with the advice, Sahib," Jamil muttered impatiently. He wanted to try it again—and again and again—until he got it right. Mr. Smith moved the boat out until the rope was fully extended. Jamil gave him the thumbs-up and they were off one more time.

It seemed to happen slower this time. Jamil focused on each step and movement of his body, making certain he didn't rush anything. When he popped up onto the surface of the water, he told himself that he didn't have to move out of the crouch quickly. He could use the entire lake if he wanted. It didn't take that long, but giving himself the time made it easier to come out of the crouch and stand.

"Woooo!" Jamil yelled. He gave his dad another thumbs-up sign. Mr. Smith returned it. Jamil kept his knees slightly bent and leaned heavily onto his back foot. He was riding between two awesome wakes. He glanced to his left and right. He hesitated for a couple of seconds. Even though the summer before he was able to catch radical air and even pulled off a half-cab a couple of times, he felt like it was all new. He wasn't sure what his body would do when he came across that wake.

Finally, he just leaned to backside and shot over the left wake. He then cut back with a smooth progressive edge and made a solid pop. He rose about three feet into the air and landed hard halfway on the opposite wake. His head and shoulders jerked forward, pulling him off balance. But he kept his knees bent, sat back on his board, and recovered. A wave of relief washed across him like spray from the boat's wake.

With each pass, Jamil's confidence increased until it had fully returned. Now the boat was heading for shore in front of the hotel. He spotted a couple of people sitting on the dock watching him. Now was the time to try a two-wake 180, Jamil thought. He cut a good edge and popped air off the first wake. Keeping the handle close to his body, he began his rotation. Unfortunately, he threw his shoulders back when he came off the wake and lost his axis. His body drifted left and he landed on his side.

"We better get back," Mr. Smith said as he pulled alongside Jamil. He looked at his watch. "It's almost time if everything keeps to the schedule you set."

"Thanks, Dad," Jamil said as he climbed back in the boat. A real sense of relief washed over him. For the first time in weeks his body didn't feel like some oversized suit of clothes. Out of control.

"HELP! I'VE BEEN ROBBED!" The sound of Naomi's screeching voice coming through the door to

Jamil's room was music to their ears. Jamil, Nat, Wall, and Kevin had gathered in Jamil's room while he changed out of his suit. As Naomi stress-tested the ears of the hotel's guests, the kids gave each other high fives.

"Shall we join her?" Jamil said dramatically. He swung wide his door and his friends followed him into the hallway.

"Oh, no! My diamond necklace has been stolen!" Naomi sobbed as she fell to her knees in hysterics. The hall was filling with guests.

"The chase is on!" someone shouted. People crowded around Naomi.

Naomi screamed one more time and violently sobbed.

Nat groaned. "I thought I told her to act angry, not so much like a helpless victim."

"She's improvising," Wall said dryly.

"Well, she's got my vote for an Oscar in the overacting category," replied Nat. She dug her hands into her pockets and tried to disappear into the woodwork.

"The shoe is planted under Naomi's window, right?" Wall whispered to his friends.

"Yeah, I took care of it last night," Jamil replied.

People were crowding around Naomi asking her questions. Doors along the hallway were opening and shutting. The excitement of the chase filled the air.

At this point Jamil stepped forward. "Okay, detectives! Attention please. As you all know, we have a robbery. Now it's your job to solve the…"

"I'VE BEEN ROBBED!" Another voice from the other end of the hall shattered the electricity of the guest sleuths. Everyone's head jerked around.

Dave Resnick, Wake Ever's creative genius, stood alone at the end of the hallway. His briefcase was turned upside down and a few stray papers were drifting out of it to the floor. "Someone has broken into my room!"

"What?" Wall blurted. "Jamil, you didn't add another mystery, did you?"

"No way," Jamil replied. "This has nothing to do with our mystery."

"Call the police! This is not a joke!" Resnick continued. He threw his leather briefcase against the wall.

"Come on. Let's find out what this is about," Kevin said as he ran down the hall.

"Excellent! There are two mysteries, not one," someone said excitedly.

"We're getting real bang for our buck!" a woman added as she hurried down the hall to interview Mr. Resnick.

"No! No!" Mr. Resnick protested as he was surrounded. "This is *real*! I really was robbed!"

"A real robbery?" Nat gasped.

Thump! Thump! Thump! Bob came racing down the hall. "Calm down, everyone," he shouted in a very uncalm way. "I'll take care of this. It's not part of the mystery weekend." He turned to Jamil. "Could you get everyone distracted by the mystery game so I can sort this out?"

Jamil nodded. "Attention, everyone!" He held up his

hands. "You need to begin your investigation. Remember, time is of the utmost importance. You must solve the crime by six-thirty tonight."

The guests followed Jamil to the lobby where Naomi was waiting on the couch. He stood beside Naomi and spoke. "Naomi is available for interviews here for the next hour. Her room, which is Room 132, will be open for inspection all morning. I advise you to begin in these two places. Look for clues. Try to make connections. Investigate!"

Naomi sat with her legs crossed, her pink, high-heeled foot bobbing up and down. The X-crew left the guests to their own devices and made their way straight back to the hallway.

"It looks like we've got our own mystery to solve," Kevin said with excitement. "You read my mind," Nat replied.

At the door to Mr. Resnick's room, Bob, Mr. Yardley, and Mr. Resnick were gathered.

"Spill it, Dave," Mr. Yardley said. "If we don't get these plans back, we're sunk."

Mr. Resnick sighed. "Okay." He turned to Bob. "The plans for next season's model were stolen from my room. This design was going to revolutionize the sport."

"But not if another manufacturer gets a copy of the plans…" interrupted Yardley.

"We have to get the plans back before someone has a chance to copy them," insisted Resnick.

The crew stood there dumbstuck as they listened.

Just then, Wall noticed the door across the hall cracked. It was Kyle. He was eavesdropping!

Wall nudged his friends. Why would Kyle be hiding? Wall decided to find out. "Kyle, why don't you come out. You should hear this, too."

Startled, Kyle opened his door. "What happened?" he asked innocently. April followed him into the hallway.

"What's wrong?" April asked.

Yardley explained what was robbed. "We've got to get the plans back."

"They couldn't have been taken from the property," Bob deducted. "No one's left since you arrived. If we act fast, we can get them back before there's damage." Bob shrugged. "Who knows? You might have just misplaced them."

"Not a chance," Resnick insisted. He held up his briefcase. "They were locked in here and I hadn't taken them out."

"Did you remember to bring them?" Kevin asked.

Resnick gave Kevin an impatient look. "Of course I did."

"Well, I suggest we hold off on calling the police," Bob said. He ran his hand nervously through his hair. "I'm sure you don't want the publicity when we might be able to get the plans back." A bead of sweat slid down the side of his face.

Yardley started to protest, but Resnick quickly cut him off. "Good idea," Resnick said. "I'm sure we can find these plans ourselves."

"Excellent," Bob replied.

The crew stood there stunned. Why wouldn't they call the police? Why wouldn't Resnick want the police to come in? Bad publicity seems like a really flimsy excuse when the fate of an entire company was on the line.

5

Nat and Jamil settled on the large bed in Jamil's room while Kevin and Wall snagged the chairs. Jamil's dad leaned against the windowsill. The sounds of the amateur detectives investigating the ground below Naomi's window drifted in. Someone exclaiming that they'd found a shoe rose above the other voices.

Inside the room the kids were barely aware of the noises outside. Their focus was on the real mystery.

"That was really strange," Nat commented. She sat with her legs crossed at the foot of the bed. "It would make sense to call the police."

"Yeah, but I guess they're worried about this getting out," Jamil countered. Jamil had piled the pillows against the headboard and was comfortably nestled among them.

"Maybe, but I didn't like the way Bob insisted on not reporting it so quickly," Kevin replied. He tipped his chair back against the wall. "And Mr. Resnick's quick

42

agreement also seemed weird. Do you think we should check them out? Maybe they could be involved in the crime."

Mr. Smith crossed his arms and watched his son and his son's friends.

"What about Kyle?" Jamil asked. He stared at the ceiling as he thought through the scenario. "He was eavesdropping on the whole thing. And remember those papers from Splash Boards? He lied about them. Said they were catalogs. Nat and I wondered if he might be switching sponsors. How grateful would Splash Boards be for the secret plans to the hottest new design break-through in wakeboarding?"

"You've got a point," Wall conceded. He rubbed his chin.

The room was silent for a few moments as everyone ran the events of the last hour through their minds.

As Jamil thought, the smell of mildew tickled his nose. "I just had another idea. I hate to say it, but I've noticed that this hotel is a little run-down."

"But didn't you say that shouldn't be a surprise?" Nat asked Mr. Smith.

"Well, I wasn't surprised," Mr. Smith conceded. "I mean, getting a place like this ready after it's been closed for a couple of months takes a lot of work. And it isn't like the entire place is booked for a convention. It's just a special weekend for a small group of people."

"Would you have the place in perfect order?" Jamil asked his dad.

Mr. Smith shrugged. "I would hope to, but you can't always predict what's going to get in the way."

"No kidding." Nat laughed. "Like a real mystery crashing the fake one."

"Yeah," Kevin argued, picking up Jamil's point, "but we have to consider that there is a reason Bob couldn't get the place in perfect shape." He rubbed his fingers through his hair. "Maybe he's having money troubles, so he couldn't afford to."

"I'm not following. What's this have to do with the stolen plans?" Wall asked as he sat forward in his chair.

"What if Bob stole the plans either to sell them to another company or to ransom them back to Wake Ever?" Kevin suggested. "That would be a pretty quick way to raise a bundle of cash and get this place fixed up."

Wall snorted. "That's pretty far-fetched. I'm more inclined to think Resnick stole them before I would consider Bob."

"Why?" Jamil asked.

"Maybe Resnick hates his job. Maybe he wants to sell the plans or use them as leverage for a raise," Wall explained. "It would be a perfect cover, saying the plans were stolen."

"And he did seem to jump rather quickly on Bob's suggestion about not calling the police," Nat added.

"You've got a point," Kevin replied. "But do we really have time to investigate this? Remember, we *are* running our own mystery."

Jamil glanced around the room. "Should we cancel it?"

"No," Wall said quickly. "Let's use our mystery as a cover to investigate the real one. It will keep everyone distracted while we track down the thief."

Nat hopped off the bed. "Then we better read our Interpol fax to the amateur sleuths." She pulled a piece of paper out of her pocket.

"You guys are incredible," Mr. Smith said shaking his head in disbelief. "If you spent this much energy on schoolwork, Jamil, you'd have perfect grades."

"School isn't nearly as interesting," Jamil replied as he followed his friends out of the room.

"I'll go to Naomi's room," Jamil told his friends. He backtracked a couple of doors to Room 132. The door was open and half a dozen people were inside. "Excuse me, detectives!"

The guests laughed at what Jamil called them.

"An important piece of information has been discovered in the lobby," explained Jamil. Everyone hurried from the room.

Jamil went over to the window and leaned out. There were still a couple of people searching for more clues outside the room. "You better go to the lobby. An important announcement concerning the robbery is about to be made."

"Thanks," a woman with a black ponytail said. She and her friend headed for the porch.

The lobby hummed with expectation. Everyone was looking at Nat, Jamil, Kevin, and Wall.

Jamil elbowed Kevin. "You do it."

Kevin shook his head. "No, you."

Nat grabbed the paper and said, "I'll do it, wimps." She pulled a desk chair away from a writing table and climbed on it. Now everyone in the room could see her. She coughed to get her audience's attention. Then in a very officious voice, she said, "We've just received a fax from Interpol, the international police." She held out the piece of paper with a flourish. "It's seems we have a famous jewel thief in our midsts. This fax explains that the Phantom, the world's most sought-after jewel thief, has been tracked down to this hotel. The authorities are on their way, but won't arrive until tonight. The police recommend that everyone hide their jewelry until they arrive."

"What's he look like?" someone asked.

Nat made like she was reading the fax again. "There's no description. It says no one has seen him, but there is a rumor that he has a tattoo on his hand. A diamond."

Bob stood behind the front desk with a wide grin on his face.

"I know who it is!" one guy shouted.

"Who? Who?" asked others frantically.

"No way! I'm not telling," he cried as he ran out of the hotel. "Now all I have to do is tie him to the robbery."

"Everyone show their hands," a guy in a red running suit commanded.

Surprisingly, everyone did it.

Nat smiled with satisfaction.

"Where's Nick?" Jamil asked quietly.

"I think he's out on the dock," Kevin answered.

Wall walked over to the window. "Nope. He's riding on the lake. I think Kyle is driving the boat."

Jamil came up behind him. "Fresh! He can carve it."

Nick had made a deep progressive toeside carve, shifting his weight onto his front foot and giving his rear hand a little extra pull. He came at the wake like a bullet and popped high in the air. With a pull of his front hand, he twisted a 180. Using he head and shoulders to lead his rotation, he front-rolled to *revert*. His lead hand swung low to his side to help with the balance.

"Stylin' *scarecrow*," Wall gasped.

Kevin was more concerned with the real mystery. "Did anyone think to check Mr. Resnick's door for tampering?"

They all shook their heads.

"Let's do it," Jamil said. They headed toward Mr. Resnick's room.

At the door, Wall kneeled and examined the doorjamb and lock. He ran his fingers over the gap where the door met the frame. It was smooth and unmarked.

Nat leaned over his shoulder to see for herself.

"Would you mind?" Wall said impatiently. "You're blocking the light."

Nat took a step back.

Wall examined the keyhole from several different angles. "This lock looks fine. There are no scratches. No one's tampered with it."

"Then how'd the person break in?" Nat wondered.

"That is, if they broke in," Kevin reminded her.

"Maybe the perp had a pass key. Or get this, maybe they entered through the window just like our thief!"

"That would be so cool if the real theft mirrored the fake one," Jamil cracked.

Wall knocked on Mr. Resnick's door. "Might as well check his room out since we're here."

A moment later, the door to the room opened. Mr. Resnick stood there with a questioning look.

"Could we examine your room for clues? I think we might find something," Wall explained.

Mr. Resnick laughed.

"What's so funny?" Jamil asked with confusion.

"You kids are. Give me a break." He continued to laugh. "Just because you're running a mystery game doesn't mean you can solve a real one."

"But I think we might be able to help," Kevin protested.

"Don't worry," Mr. Resnick said. "We've got everything under control. You kids run and play." He shut the door.

The crew could hear him talking to someone in the room. They couldn't make out what he or the other person were saying, but they were certain it was more jokes about them.

Nat banged her hand against the wall in frustration. "I can't stand grown-ups not taking me seriously. We'll show them."

Just then, Wimple, the resort's handyman, came out of Kyle's room.

Ignoring the kids, Wimple headed down the hall and turned right, toward the lobby. As he turned, Jamil noticed a partially concealed envelope in his right hand.

Jamil grabbed Nat's and Kevin's shirtsleeves and dragged them after him. "Wall, come on."

Wondering what Jamil was suddenly excited about, they followed him into the lobby. Jamil stopped. He had lost sight of Wimple.

Guests milled about, busily investigating.

Then Jamil spotted Wimple through the window on the porch. Wimple was walking down the steps. "Hurry!" Jamil called to his friends.

On the porch the crew watched Wimple cross the parking lot to an ATV with *Lake Potow Resort* written on its side.

"What? What are we supposed to be watching?" Nat asked.

Wall nodded to Wimple in the ATV backing out of the parking space. "Him?"

"Didn't you see the envelope in Wimple's hand as he left Kyle's room?" Jamil asked with excitement. "I think the mystery has just been solved!"

6

"All I need to do is find out who has the match to that shoe we found under the window," a guy in blue jean cut-offs said to his friend. Both were standing on the porch just down from the X-crew.

The friend glanced inside. "I'd say about half the guys here wear a size ten. I know I do."

"Me too," the first guy groaned. "We need to find another clue or we'll never figure this out."

Kevin glanced over at the two. "Looks like our mystery is going well. Wait till they find that shoe in the garbage."

They all laughed, except Jamil. Panic flushed his face.

"Uh… guys…" he stuttered. "I forgot to put the shoe in the garbage can."

"What?" Nat cried. "You were supposed to do that last night so people might find it in the morning."

"I know. I know. I just forgot. I had to wait a half

hour for Lars to show up, and by then I was really beat and I just forgot," Jamil explained.

"Let's just take care of it," Kevin responded. The crew went directly to Jamil's room. The shoe was perched on the TV.

Jamil reached to grab it, but his hand worked more like a catcher's mitt. The shoe slipped through his fingers and fell to the floor.

"Hurry up, butterfingers," Nat said impatiently.

Jamil cringed. He thought he was over his clumsiness thing. "How are people going to find this shoe? Is it really important for it to be found?" Jamil asked.

"You mean, it's like a Cinderella thing," Wall said. He understood what Jamil was talking about. "All the guests really need is one shoe. Then they can have everyone try it on to see who it fits."

"What if the shoe size fits half the guests here?" Nat said. "We already know it fits Nick, Mr. Cousins, and Lars. Who knows how many other men staying here are a size ten? We didn't measure people's feet when they arrived, you know." Her blond ponytail bobbed impatiently.

"The point of planting the other shoe is to give the guests an extra clue," Kevin explained. "Their first two suspects will probably be Nick and Mr. Cousins. Now, Nick, they would think, doesn't even own a pair of dress shoes. He's a totally casual kind of guy. And Mr. Cousins is so classy that he wouldn't wear dress shoes with thick rubber soles. This will lead them to the logical conclusion that the only other person who would wear dress shoes at a hotel is an employee."

"This is a resort," Jamil countered with a smirk. "Dinners are pretty formal. Everyone here should have a pair of dress shoes."

"These folks are a bunch of wakeboarder dudes, Jamil." Nat laughed. "We're lucky they wear shoes to dinner at all!"

"Besides," continued Kevin, "Lars's feet are different sizes. This other shoe is an eleven. This is the final clue that will lead them directly to him. So we have to plant the shoe or the guests will never figure it out."

"Okay, let's do it," Jamil conceded. He marched out of the room carrying the shoe in a bag. They headed outside toward the back of the hotel where the garbage bins were. "The guests better get that whoever owned the first shoe they found will want to dump the other one. Otherwise, they might not think to search the garbage."

"I'm not worried," Nat said. "These guys are really smart. I heard some people already saying they wanted to search the grounds for the second shoe. They'll find it."

The crew stopped in front of the sturdy metal bins. The lids were latched shut to keep any furry creatures from breaking in. As they opened the cans up, a horrible odor wafted up.

"Oh, gross," Kevin exclaimed. "This is definitely not my favorite part of the job." Dozens of flies swarmed above a large plastic bag that was torn open.

"Last night's dinner," Nat gagged. She pointed to

hunks of blackened and yellowed food spilling from the plastic bag. "Yum."

"This is rude," Wall agreed. "Put the shoe on top so the guests won't have to go digging too far. We don't want to be sued if they get sick from the fumes."

As Jamil, helped the shoe over the garbage can, trying not to breathe too deep, he noticed a piece of paper. "Hey, guys, look at this." He pointed at what looked like a letter addressed to Splash Boards.

Kevin gingerly pulled out the letter while plugging his nose. As soon as he had it out, Jamil dropped the shoe and slammed down the lid. He latched the can tight.

"What's it say?" Nat asked impatiently.

Kevin carefully unfolded the paper. He held it at the edges to avoid the banana goo smeared all over it. "It's addressed to Splash Boards. And it says…" He quickly scanned the letter. "It says this person wants to start a partnership with them." Kevin read further. "He would like to meet with them next week to discuss the terms. He thinks they'll really like what he can bring to their fine business estblishment. And it's signed… Evan!"

"This seems important, but what does it mean?" Wall asked.

"Well," Nat suggested, "we did think Evan was looking for a sponsor. Maybe Wake Ever turned him down, so now he's seeing if Splash Boards is interested. We should hang on to this, but right now we need to talk to Wimple. Find out what he was carrying this morning. He should be back by now."

"This certainly doesn't tie Kyle to the robbery," Kevin said. "But it could mean something."

The kids turned to go back into the hotel. They needed Wimple to tie this mystery together. As they were headed toward the door, they overheard some guests.

"We need to find the matching shoe," a blond woman said. "You know the theif got rid of it, but maybe something about it would lead us to him."

"Or her," countered her companion. "Where should we look?"

"The garbage?" suggested the blond woman.

"Yuck! Rooting around in a bunch of stinky trash is not how I expected to spend my vacation. But if it'll get me that new board, I'll do it."

The kids smiled at each other. They were so good! If they ever got tired of being real sleuths, they could do this for a living. As they walked up the porch steps, they heard the women shout, "Oh, man, this stuff is nasty!... Look! It's the shoe!"

The door slammed behind them. Wall ambled over to the front desk where Lars was pretending to be busy. "Get ready, friend, the detectives will be onto you soon. Have you been walking around, so folks can see you're wearing different shoes than yesterday?"

Nat, Jamil, and Kevin came over.

"Of course," replied Lars. "I even commented about how comfortable my feet were finally. Any astute individual would have noticed I'm not wearing the proper shoes for my position."

"Great job!" Nat exclaimed.

Wall glanced at the clock behind the desk. "It's almost time for Kyle's exhibition."

"Why don't we split up then?" Kevin suggested. Two of us can make sure the rumor spreads that they found the other shoe and the other two look for Wimple."

"Good idea," Jamil said. "Nat, you come with me. We'll talk to Wimple."

The crew split up.

A few minutes later, Jamil and Nat found Bob in the kitchen peeling potatoes. He was an expert with that peeler. Potato peels flew everywhere. There was no sign of Wimple. By the stove, Bob's wife, Maggie, was wearing a white chef's hat. She was stirring something in a large stainless-steel pot.

"Hey! How's the mystery going?" Bob asked.

"Which one? The fake one is doing great, but the real one is a little more difficult," Jamil replied. "Have you guys had any luck finding the plans?"

"No," Bob answered. "Joe and Dave are looking right now. I've told my cleaning staff to keep their eyes peeled when they're cleaning the guests' rooms. But if nothing shows up, we'll have to take more drastic measures."

"Could we ask you a question about Wimple?" Nat said tentatively. She needed information, but she didn't want to say anything bad about Wimple to Bob. He might clam up because he really seems to like him.

"Shoot," said Bob.

"Well," continued Jamil, "do you think there's anyway

he could be involved in the robbery?"

Bob snorted. "You've got to be kidding me. Wimple?"

"Yes, Wimple," Nat replied anxiously. "We saw him take an envelope from Kyle's room this morning and leave for town. If he's in on it with Kyle, he might have been taking the plans so they wouldn't be found."

"You see," Jamil tried to explain, "we think Kyle is jumping sponsors—from Wake Ever to Splash Boards. If he is, it gives him a motive to steal the plans."

"He needed Wimple, though, to get him into Mr. Resnick's room so he could pull off the plan," Nat added.

Bob shook his head. "You've got Wimple wrong. I sent him to town to pick up supplies and drop off the mail. He went to everyone's room and asked if they had any mail to send."

"So the envelope might not have come from Kyle's room?" Jamil asked.

"That's right. He could have picked it up from someone else, or it could have come from anyone. Who knows? You'll have to speak to Wimple. He should be back soon." Bob continued. "One thing is for sure. Wimple is not in any conspiracy with anyone."

"We're back at square one," Jamil said with disappointment.

"Not quite," Nat countered. "Just because Wimple isn't involved doesn't mean Kyle isn't. He or someone else could have sent out the plans with Wimple. We just have to ask Wimple who gave him that envelope and any others."

Suddenly the pot behind Maggie, who had been listening intently to the conversation, boiled over. The hissing sound of liquid turning to steam on the burner interupted everything. Maggie turned down the flame underneath the pot. "I hope I didn't burn it."

"What is it?" Jamil asked. He had forgotten to eat breakfast that morning and now his stomach growled.

"Vegetable soup for lunch," Maggie answered. She blew on a spoonful of soup and tasted it. "Still good." She smiled.

"If lunch is going to be ready, we've got to get to work," Bob said. "I don't want empty stomachs making any of the Wake Ever people cranky."

"Yes, we don't want them deciding not to stop here on their tour because they were hungry," Maggie said with an edge of humor.

"We get the hint," Jamil said. "We want to catch Kyle's exhibition, so we'll get out of your hair."

Down by the lake, guests had gathered along the beach. They were watching Kyle's performance. April had set up a sound system to play music, and was stacking CDs that she would play to accent Kyle's gnarly moves.

"Have you guys heard this?" April asked Nat and Jamil as they approached. She held up a CD case for a group called Funkdoodle Bug. "It's really great."

"Put it on," Nat said with excitement. "Who's driving the boat?"

"Joe and Dave," April replied. "I'm stuck playing DJ."

"There's Wall and Kevin." Jamil pointed to an spot on the beach where they sat. Most of the guests were either in boats out in the cove or on the dock. "Come on." He and Nat ran over.

"Have we missed anything?" Nat asked as she sat down on a bed of smooth pebbles.

"No. It's just about to start, I think," Kevin answered. He glanced over at the dock where Kyle was standing with his all-black wakeboard. Joe Yardley and Dave Resnick were in the boat.

"Looks like he's going to do a dock start," Wall said as the motorboat moved slowly out into the cove without Kyle in it.

Kyle sat on the dock's edge and slipped his feet in his high wraps. He picked up the handle. When the rope was taut, Kyle signaled the boat to go. It took off with a monstrous roar. Kyle quickly slipped off the dock and dipped low into the water. Like a deep-water start, he was crouched with his knees in his chest and his elbows buried into his stomach. With his board sideways in the start position, he leaned radically back to force the water to support him. Slowly, he came out of the crouch and lengthened his arms.

"Did you guys find out anything from Wimple?" Wall asked.

"No," replied Jamil. "He's not back from town yet. We did talk to Bob, though. He insists Wimple couldn't be involved. He told us he had Wimple ask all the guests if they had any mail they needed taken into town. That envelope could have come from anybody."

"Well, we'll just have to wait until Wimple gets back and ask him for a list of anyone who gave him anything," said Kevin. "That'll at least narrow down the suspects— if the plans were among his deliveries."

"I wish our real mystery was as straightforward as our fake one," Jamil commented as he sat back on his hands.

"Maybe it is," Kevin replied. "I mean, the fake mystery seems simple because we made it up, but the guests probably don't think it's so obvious. With the red herrings we've thrown in, most of them will get distracted and not see the real one."

"We need to look at this mystery more closely," Nat suggested. She drew her knees up to her chin and wrapped her arms around them.

"How?" Jamil asked with a certain feeling of frustration.

"Well, let's start by coming up with a list of suspects," Kevin said.

Wall began to tick off names with his fingers. "There's Bob. There's Mr. Resnick. There's Kyle. Who do you want to start with?"

"Don't forget the rest of the guests," Jamil added, somewhat dispirited.

"I don't think we have to worry about the other guests right now," Nat replied. "They didn't even know that Mr. Resnick had the plans. I think we can stick to people who might have known this."

"But that's exactly the trap we're trying to lead the

guests into," Jamil complained. "To make them focus on the obvious suspects."

"You're right," Kevin said. "But before we can expand our list of suspects we need to eliminate the most obvious."

The crew's attention was drawn away from their discussion for a few minutes by an amazing sequence of tricks performed by Kyle. As he dug his board into the water, almost stopping his momentum, he suddenly lifted his rear foot, and pushed off the water with his toes. From there he performed a whirlybird. His board rolled over his head, his arms flew out sideways like they were wings, and he stuck the landing so solidly that he was able to move back to the wake for a speedball.

"That takes superhuman power," Wall gasped.

Kyle then shot across the trough and over the opposite wake to air a backside 360. For some reason, he didn't stick it and wiped out with a huge splash.

"Oh, man! Wipeout," Kevin exclaimed. "No one could have pulled off those three tricks in a row. Your muscles can't take it." He turned back to his friends. "So who seems the most likely suspect?"

"Kyle," Nat, Jamil, and Wall answered together.

"Why?" Kevin prodded.

"He has the most to gain by stealing the plans," Jamil replied. "He could take the plans to Splash Boards."

Kevin held up his hand like a traffic cop. "Wait. You're jumping to conclusions. All we know is that Kyle got mail from Splash Boards and maybe lied about what was in the envelope."

"We also know that April is really angry at him," Nat added. "Remember, last night we overheard them arguing about a business decision that Kyle was going to make."

"That's true," Kevin admitted. "So this leads us to think that Kyle might be switching sponsors. How does this lead us to the conclusion that he stole the plans? Any other evidence?"

"Okay, teacher, I'll bite," Wall cracked. "We saw Wimple leaving Kyle's room with an envelope to mail right after the plans were stolen."

"Good," Kevin replied, taking on a fake teacherly voice.

"Ugh! Now you sound like Mrs. Constanine," Nat cried in mock disgust. Mrs. Constanine was the math teacher at Hoke Valley Middle School where they attended seventh and eighth grades.

Everyone laughed.

"Okay," Kevin said catching his breath. "None of these things directly connect Kyle to the robbery. They just suggest that he might have a motive."

"What about Bob?" Nat asked.

"I really don't think Bob is a very viable suspect," Jamil cut in. "It seems he'd benefit more if this weekend went smoothly. Then the tour would come next year and he'd have a foothold in the summer business."

"Good point," Kevin said. "But what if Bob is in more trouble than we think? He could steal the plans and either sell them to another company or ransom them back to Wake Ever to get them to sign a long-term sponsorship contract."

"He did suggest not calling the police," Wall reminded everyone. "Maybe he doesn't want the robbery to be investigated."

"It's possible," Jamil conceded. "But it seems kind of farfetched."

"One person we haven't talked about is Resnick," Kevin added. "He had access to the plans. He could have faked the robbery. Didn't he want to avoid calling the police, too?"

The others nodded.

"But Mr. Resnick was really upset this morning," Nat countered.

Kevin sighed. "You're right. I thought he was really upset, too." He looked at his friends for any other suggestions.

They all just looked out onto the lake where Kyle was turning the wake behind the motorboat into a launchpad for a space shuttle takeoff.

"I don't think we have any evidence tying anyone to the robbery," Jamil finally said. "What we need to do is somehow flush out the thief, so that he'll reveal himself."

"Or herself," Nat reminded everyone.

Their discussion lapsed into silence with this suggestion and their attention centered back on Kyle and his board magic.

With a super-progressive edge into the wake, Kyle stood tall on the board and started what looked like a run-of-the-mill *raley*, but at the peak he moved effortlessly it into a *krypt* where he rotated to *fakie*.

"He's got to be tired," Jamil exclaimed. Kyle had been riding for half an hour already.

But Kyle wasn't ready to give it up yet. He surged across both wakes to the opposite side and cut back with a deep edge that looked like he was going into another raley. When he hit the wake, however, he flew into a scarecrow and raised his arms in the air as he let go of the rope. Slowly, he sunk back into the water and the motor boat circled to pick him up.

"Hey!" Jamil shouted. "I've got it!"

"What?" Wall asked.

"I know a way we can flush out the perp," Jamil answered. "First we need to…" *Snap!*

Jamil spun around. Evan was standing just a few feet behind them.

"I'll tell you later," Jamil whispered.

"Hey! Wimple's back," Wall said as he watched the Lake Potow ATV pull into the parking lot. Most of the guests had already gone up to the hotel for lunch. The crew was waiting for Mr. Yardley and Mr. Resnick to wrap things up. Jamil had a plan to trap the thief that involved Wake Ever, so he wanted to spring it on them right away.

"Someone should talk to him," Jamil said, torn between wanting to interview Wimple and needing to talk to Yardley and Resnick.

"I'll do it," Wall volunteered. "You guys wait for them." He nodded toward the dock and then rushed up the bank of the shore. He ran barefoot across the parking lot. It was easy to catch up to Wimple since he moved at a speed of about six feet an hour.

Shoulders hunched from carrying a heavy box of supplies, Wimple staggered across the parking lot. He had left the hatch open to unload other boxes as well.

"Excuse me, sir," Wall called.

Wimple froze, but didn't turn.

"I wanted to ask you about the mail you took into town today," Wall said.

Sweat dripped off the tip of Wimple's nose like a leaky faucet. He stood there silent for moment as if Wall were speaking Greek. Then he coughed and replied, "Yes." He took two hesitant steps toward the front porch.

Wall put his hand gently on Wimple's arm to stop him.

Wimple dropped the box he was carrying. "Oh, my," he grunted. The back of his hand brushed across his nose and he bent over to gather the two cans of caviar and three bottles of champagne.

"Let me help you," Wall said as he knelt beside Wimple. He grabbed one of the bottles. "This is pretty fancy stuff. Is the hotel serving champagne and caviar tonight?"

"Oh, no," Wimple said with a chuckle. "This is a special order."

"By whom?" Wall asked gently, not wanting to push too far.

"Mr. Rodriguez asked me to pick this up in town," Wimple explained.

Wall reached over and grabbed the box from Wimple. "Let me take this inside for you." He glanced back at the open hatch of the car. "It looks like you've got more to bring in."

"Thanks," Wimple said with obvious relief.

"Oh, and one more thing," Wall said casually. "Speaking of Mr. Rodriguez. Did he give you an envelope this morning?"

Wimple nodded his head. "Yes. Yes, he did."

"Oh," Wall replied. He tried to think quick to pump Wimple for more information. "Do you remember who it was addressed to? Kyle said something to me about contacting the same company that he had sent the envelope to, but I can't remember what the name of it was."

Wimple thought for a moment. "It was Splash something. I don't know. You'll have to ask Mr. Rodriguez."

Wall nodded. "Thanks for your help. I'll get these inside right away."

"To the kitchen," Wimple called after him.

After dropping off the box, Wall went through the kitchen doors into the dining room. Everyone was seated for lunch. Mr. Yardley and Mr. Resnick were standing at the front of the room and seemed to be about to make an announcement. Jamil, Nat, and Kevin were standing behind them.

"We have an important announcement to make," Mr. Yardley said above the din of conversation.

The room quieted.

"For those of you who heard about Wake Ever's robbery this morning, there's nothing to worry about." Mr. Yardley beamed with confidence. "It turns out the plans that were stolen were actually flawed. Dave and I discovered these flaws as we were trying to recreate the plans this morning."

The announcement caught Wall by surprise. But when he saw his friends standing behind Mr. Yardley, he muttered, "So that's what you were up to, Jamil." He hurried over.

"So whoever stole the plans, they're worthless," Mr. Yardley concluded. "Enjoy your lunch and good luck on the mystery game you all came to participate in." Scattered applause and a few laughs swept across the room. Wall snaked through the spaced tables toward his friends, who had gathered at the same table as the night before.

"Cool plan." Wall grinned. "It's got to work."

"I hope," Jamil replied. "We don't have much else otherwise."

"I've got something, too," Wall said as he slid into his seat.

"What?" his three friends asked.

"Wimple told me that the envelope *was* for Splash Boards," Wall explained. "And it was from Kyle."

"I knew it," Nat said as she slammed her fist into her hand.

"And that's not all," Wall continued. "Wimple was bringing in caviar and champagne. Kyle had made a special request for it."

"So Kyle's planning on celebrating something," Kevin concluded. "It must be the stolen plans."

"Well, now we can confront him," Jamil suggested. "He'll think the plans are a bust and we can trap him into admitting he stole them." Jamil glanced across the room where Kyle and April were sitting with a few guests.

"It makes perfect sense," Nat added. "Nobody but

Kyle really stands to benefit from them as much."

At that moment, Lars came through the kitchen doors with a tray on his shoulder. He was still wearing the sneakers.

"I hope someone notices," Kevin said as he watched Lars unload the bowls of vegetable soup at a table nearby.

"Give the laborer his food before his sweat is dry," Mr. Smith said as he sat in the remaining empty chair. "I'm hungry." He shook his napkin out and laid it on his lap. "How have your labors been going so far?"

"The mystery seems to be going fine," Jamil replied. "And I think we just might have cornered the thief who stole the plans."

Mr. Smith grinned. "I knew recommending you guys wouldn't be a mistake." Lars set the bowls around the table and everyone dug in.

After lunch Mr. Smith went out onto the porch to read while the crew watched Kyle and April finish their lunch across the room.

"Look, they're alone," Nat said as the last person at Kyle and April's table left. "Let's talk to them now."

As they passed tables of diners, they could hear guests quizzing Naomi, Mr. Cousins, and Nick.

Jamil noticed Mr. Cousins lean toward the people at his table and in a stage whisper say, "I wouldn't be surprised if Naomi stole her own necklace. She does live beyond her means, you know."

At another table, Nick said loudly, "I'm retired. Been retired for a while."

The crew smiled at each other with a sense of satisfaction. The pretend mystery was now taking care of itself. They could focus on wrapping up the lose ends of the real mystery.

"Do you mind if we join you?" Jamil asked as they approached Kyle and April.

April smiled. "Please." She waved her hand at the empty seats. "Did you enjoy Kyle's exhibition?"

"You ruled," Wall told Kyle.

"I couldn't believe how many tricks you did out there," Kevin said. "I can't believe you can still stand."

Kyle laughed. "I'm pretty sore, but I'll be fine for this afternoon's clinic. You guys coming?"

"You bet," Jamil answered. He was amped to ride now that he knew his body was following his orders again. Then Jamil paused. "But we didn't come over to talk about that."

"What?" Kyle asked with curiousity. He put his elbows on the table.

Like with most difficult conversations, Jamil wasn't sure how to start. Finally, he just waded in. "Well, we're pretty sure now who stole the plans."

"Who?" April asked excitedly.

"You sent a package this morning to Splash Boards," Jamil explained. "We believe Wake Ever's plans were in that envelope. We believe you stole the plans as part of your deal to jump to Splash Boards."

"Boy, have you guys made a mistake," April interrupted. "That envelope contained the *un*signed contract that Splash Boards sent to Kyle."

"That's right. I'm not leaving Wake Ever," Kyle explained.

"But we heard you guys arguing last night," Nat countered.

"You sure did," Kyle continued. "And that was what made up my mind. If April was against it, then I couldn't do it. You see…," he glanced at April. "We're getting married in a month, so the last thing I want is for her to be mad at me."

"He's telling the truth," April insisted.

"Besides, Wake Ever has done good by me," added Kyle.

"I don't get it," Jamil said confused. "It seemed like you *had* to be the thief."

"I guess we're starting at square one," Kevin commented with disappointment. The crew retreated to the lobby. They had to figure out what the next step was.

"I say we wait," Jamil said. "Let Yardley's announcement sink in and see what happens."

"I hate waiting," Nat said as she folded her arms across her chest. "I think I'll crawl out of my skin."

"Let's do something," Wall suggested. "Our mystery seems to be going fine. I heard Bob tell some guests that they have mountain bikes that we can borrow and there are trails going up in the hills."

"Great!" Jamil said. The crew exited the lobby. As they came onto the porch, they suddenly heard shouting.

"Get out and don't come back!"

"I don't care what you think!"

Down at the end of the porch Dave Resnick and Evan were in a shouting match.

"Leave!" Resnick commanded as he pointed to the parking lot.

"You don't own this place," Evan replied.

"Harsh," Kevin said to his friends as they went down the steps.

"The bikes are in the shed," Wall said. "Come on."

"I wonder what that's all about?" Jamil asked. "Something to do with the letter we found?"

"Could be anything," Nat replied. "Evan was bothering them last night. Maybe Mr. Resnick finally lost his patience with him."

"Maybe it's not a coincidence that they're arguing right after the announcement was made about the plans," Kevin suggested. "Maybe Evan deserves a closer look."

"Let's discuss it on the trail," Nat said, anxious to be doing something, anything.

9

The doubletrack trail started at the edge of the towering pine forest behind the hotel. Nat, Jamil, Kevin, and Wall were on the hotel's guest mountain bikes, ancient, heavy bikes with flat pedals that looked like ice cream sandwiches. Covered with a bed of dry pine needles, the trail was slippery. The five kilometer climb to the summit would be difficult and slow.

"Do we now focus on Bob or Evan?" Wall asked as they came around the first switchback.

"Let's talk about it at the top," Jamil huffed. Mountain biking was not his best sport. As he pedaled up the track, he suddenly had a rush of uneasiness. Could he handle his bike well enough to not crash? He couldn't guarantee his body would follow his commands. He'd know soon enough, he thought, when he saw three-foot-thick logs lying across the track.

Of the crew, Nat was the monster of the trails. This

past spring she had designed the trail for the Bear Claw Mountain Bike Race at Hoke Valley and was still involved in organizing other races around the state.

The crew dropped into a single file as they approached the logs. Nat led and wheelied her front tire over the first log and hopped her rear onto it so she could get traction to create enough power to ride over the second log. Kevin followed, popped his front wheel onto the log, and then came off it hard so his rear tire could climb onto the log and roll over. Wall did the same effortlessly.

When Jamil came to the log, Nat and Kevin were already past the third one and Wall was coming over the last a bit shaky, but steady enough to make it through. Jamil pulled back on his handlebars and wheelied in an attempt to mirror Nat's move. But he landed on the teeth of his chainring. He leaned forward to slide to his rear tire, but instead performed a scuzzy chainsuck. His chain slipped off the ring and left him stradled on the first log and more than a little embarrassed.

Jamil knew what had happened. He had freaked. He was so anxious about the move that he had set up impossible expectations. He wanted his body to perform perfectly, which never happened even before he had grown. In the best of times, Jamil would have been lucky to make it through the obstacle.

"Agh!" Jamil cried in frustration. He lifted his bike and carried it past the logs.

His friends slowed and glanced back at him, but they didn't say a word. They knew better than to joke with

Jamil when he was this angry.

Jamil flipped his bike over roughly and put the chain back on the ring. In a matter of seconds he was back on his bike, cranking hard in granny gear to catch up to his friends. He switched to a higher gear as he picked up speed. He and his friends were now standing on their pedals and pumping up the steady incline.

"When do we get to the top?" Wall asked, out of breath.

"Maybe a couple more kilometers," Nat said. "You want to rest?"

"Not yet," Wall answered.

"Bob did say the ride down was the sickest," Nat added as consolation.

"That's if I still have legs left by then," Jamil joked. Even though he was finding the ride frustrating, he was still amped to be on a bike on a trail. This summer was his first summer mountain biking and he had come to love it almost as much as Nat did.

They cranked steadily up the trail across wide roots and over rocks until they came to a small stream. Nat stopped and waited for her friends. She was a good two hundred feet ahead of them.

"The good thing about being first is that you get more rest time," Nat called.

"And you're the one that needs it most," Kevin cracked.

"Not!" Wall added.

"I think the top is just beyond the next switchback,"

Nat said optimistically. She could see an opening in the trees where the sun shone brightly.

"That's the best news I've had all day," Jamil huffed. He pulled up next to Nat and leaned on his handlebars.

Wall climbed back on his bike. "I hope Bob greased the bearings on these bikes." He charged into the stream. Water flew everywhere. "This feels great!" he cried as he doused himself with water.

"I'm right behind you," Jamil called. He plowed into the stream. His rear wheel bounced like a Superball™ off the smooth rocks.

Nat watched her friends. Then she lifted her bike onto her shoulder and carried it across the stream. "I'm not corroding this bike, even if it isn't mine."

Kevin followed her lead and carried his, too. "When I saw the stream, I was just grateful that the chains on our bikes hadn't destructed on the climb. I'm sure Bob doesn't lube these chains after each guest."

"You can always dream," Nat said. She stood on her pedals and quickly caught up to Jamil and Wall.

The summit was past the next switchback just like Nat had said. They all collapsed when they reached the clearing. It was a large rock that looked out on the entire valley. Jamil laid back on the hot rock and squirted water all over his face. Kevin and Wall walked to the edge and looked over the cliff. The drop was about a hundred feet. Nat stood on the highest part of the rock and sucked down water from her bottle. She stared out at the amazing view.

Two hawks circled above the trees. Their wings

spread wide, drifting on updrafts of air. The mountains on the horizon were stacked up like waves in a swell. The tops of pine trees below them led like a gentle slope to the lake's edge. For the first time the entire lake could be seen.

Jamil sat up and looked over the valley. "Hey, the lake isn't that big," he said with surprise. "I could have sworn it was much larger."

"I know," Wall said. He pointed at someone wakeboarding. "Who do you think that is?"

Kevin shrugged. "It could be anyone." The rider jumped a two wake 180. "They're pretty good though," he added.

Jamil came up beside him. "That's the exact problem we have with this robbery. It could be anyone."

"Not anymore," Nat replied. "At least we know it's not Kyle or April."

"So that leaves what? Thirty other people?" Jamil said impatiently.

"Not exactly. We do know that not everyone knew Resnick had the plans," Kevin countered. "We just have to watch and wait."

"Wait," Nat grumbled. She raised her arms to the sky and shouted, "I hate waiting! I'm keeping my eye on Evan. He's definitely weird, and that letter sounded suspicious."

"Let Yardley's announcement do its work. The thief will eventually expose himself," Jamil concluded, now a little more realistic. "Once he believes the plans are no good, he's going to make a mistake of some kind." Jamil paused. "He might even try to steal the new plans."

"We better warn Yardley and Resnick," Wall said.

"Good idea," Jamil replied.

They all stood silently for a few minutes and drank in the view. One of the hawks suddenly dove into the trees and disappeared.

"Lunch," Jamil cracked. He drank the last drops from his water bottle.

"Let's roll," Nat said. The crew climbed back on their bikes and took another, steeper trail.

Everyone shifted their weight over their back tires and flicked their brakes for control. The trail had turned into a singletrack of loose gravel, hard-packed dirt, and large rocks. They sliced and diced across some seriously technical track. The bone-rattling terrain led them down the steep track with tight switchbacks and unforgiving drop-offs.

Each rider had to start their turns wide, cut them sharp, and play the back brake with the speed and dexterity of a pinball wizard. What made it even more difficult, however, was that this slope descended into the shadows of the mountain. The late afternoon sun had already disappeared behind the summit.

Jamil slowed further behind his friends. At times the trail would seem smooth and obstacle-free, but then suddenly a sharp rock would appear like a ghost out of the shadows. He'd have to react lightning fast to avoid a brutal biff. He could just imagine the kind of facial he'd experience riding downhill over rocks and gravel. His momentum would endo him headfirst into the track. This was not the kind of trail to ride without total confidence. One hesitation. One lag in a twitch reflex, and that was it.

Jamil glanced ahead and saw Nat come off a drop at a high speed and cruise around a couple of loose, rocky outcroppings. He grit his teeth and extended his arms and legs. The saddle passed between his legs. As he shifted his weight backward, he pushed his bike forward and lifted up the front wheel. Then he stood over his pedals, moving his weight forward. He rode down the rock on his back tire. His arms and legs shuddered as they absorbed the impact of his front wheel landing, but he stayed on his bike. Triumph pulsed through him. He made a sharp turn. His rear wheel slid, but he powered through it pedaling hard. His confidence was growing as he caught up with his friends.

Nat pulled up before another steep drop. "Let's rest before we take this next one."

They were about halfway down the trail, which zigzagged above them for several hundred feet.

"I wish I hadn't stopped to look at this drop," Jamil said fearfully. "I think I might walk my bike down this one."

"I was thinking the same," Kevin said.

Suddenly, they heard a crunching, rumbling sound above them.

"Watch out!" Nat shouted as she jumped on her bike

and flew off the drop-off like a rock diver.

Above them a wall of rocks bounced directly down at them.

"Avalanche!" Jamil shouted.

Kevin and Wall were still on their bikes and they followed Nat ahead of the falling rocks.

Jamil tried to follow, but his feet missed the pedals and got caught in his bike's chain. He fell hard just as a large rock bounced on his leg and another one smashed the front tire's rim. "Agh!" Jamil cried in serious pain.

The avalanche ended as quickly as it started. Nat, Wall, and Kevin scrambled back up the trail to help their friend.

"Look!" Wall shouted as he saw the back of another rider on the trail above them turn and ride up the trail. He scrambled up the slope, but the person was long gone by the time he got there.

10

His face twisted in pain, Jamil rolled on his side and grabbed his bloody shin. "What a dufus I am," Jamil spat angrily.

Kevin kneeled by his friend. "Are you all right?" He unhooked Jamil's bike helmet and tossed it aside.

Jamil nodded. "I think." He examined his leg. There was a gash along his shin, but it wasn't deep. Blood dripped down his leg into the dust. Clods of dirt were ground into the cut. "But I should have gotten out of the way."

"How could you? Wall and I blocked you. There was no place to go but straight down," Kevin argued. The outside of the trail dropped off sharply into the tops of several trees with no chance of a soft landing.

"It's more than that," Jamil tried to explain. "The last few weeks I feel like I've borrowed somebody else's body. Growing a couple of inches has made me all thumbs and left feet."

"Well, at least you're as tall as me now," Nat said, trying to cheer him up.

Jamil growled in frustration.

"It's not your fault," added Wall.

Nat looked closely at his wound. "Nasty. I wish I had my own bike. I could have cleaned this with my first aid kit strapped to my seat post." She took the tail of her T-shirt and dabbed the cut.

"I saw a first aid kit in the shed where we got the bikes," Kevin said.

"We better get you back and clean it up, then," Nat replied.

Kevin picked Jamil's bike off the ground. "Good luck." The front rim hung on the axle by a half dozen spokes. He kicked it and the rim collapsed.

A few small rocks bounced down the slope around them.

"Hey!" Nat shouted. Nat, Jamil, and Kevin scrambled down the trail in a panic. It seemed like another avalanche was beginning.

"Oops," Wall said sheepishly as he came back down the slope. "Sorry, guys."

"You trying to finish the job?" Jamil asked.

"We've got to get you back and fast," Nat told Jamil.

"Ride my bike," Wall suggested. "I'll carry yours on my back."

Jamil winced as he stood. "I'm not sure how well I can ride."

"Does it feel broken?" Kevin asked.

Jamil shook his head. "It just hurts a lot. Did you see who was up there?"

"No," replied Wall. "But get this. There were marks in the dirt where it looked like someone had scraped the ground. Like he was pushing rocks down the mountain. That avalanche was no freak of nature."

"I can't believe somebody would do that," Nat exclaimed.

"We must have ticked somebody off," responded Kevin.

"Yeah, like the guy who stole the plans," Wall said. He glanced back up the slope. "Also, I found bike tracks up there, besides ours. And the tracks were made by the same kind of bike as ours!"

"I don't get it," Nat said.

"The person who started the avalanche must have followed us from the resort," Wall explained.

"Let's get back," Jamil said as he stepped gingerly on his leg. "It's not so bad."

In the shed by the dock, Wall knelt beside the only other bike that was there. It was sparkling clean. "This bike is too clean. It looks like our man thought he could cover his tracks by cleaning off the bike. But now it's cleaner than ours were when we picked them up. And besides, he missed a spot under the seat."

Jamil grabbed the first aid kit by the door and irrigated his wound with hydrogen peroxide. He swabbed the excess liquid with a cotton ball. Then he squirted a dab of ointment onto a large, square adhesive bandage and slapped it on his leg.

"Let's check the desk to see who signed the bike out," Nat said as she dashed for the hotel. The others followed her, Jamil more slowly.

As Nat, Wall, and Kevin headed for the desk, Jamil went to sit down. His leg hurt bad. He collapsed in one of the overstuffed reading chairs in the far corner of the room. A minute later the others came over with a look of disappointment on their faces.

"What?" Jamil asked.

Wall shook his head.

"The bike wasn't signed out," Nat said.

"Don't give up yet," Jamil said to her. "We're almost there." He slapped his fist in his hand. "We know that the thief wanted to hurt us. The big question is, who did we make so angry?"

"Well, it obviously wasn't Kyle or April," Kevin answered. "Lars said they've been down at the dock doing the clinic for the last hour."

Jamil took a deep breath. "Okay. Who then? Our only suspect right now is either Bob or Evan. Resnick doesn't seem too likely at this point."

"Evan seems most likely," Nat cut in.

Jamil thought it through. "He's the only guest who came to the weekend early. He was eavesdropping on our discussion on the beach this morning. There was that letter. And he was arguing with Resnick after lunch. Yardley's announcement must have really made him furious."

"Enough to try to kill us." Kevin gulped.

"Let's see if he's in his room." Wall leaped up and headed toward the hall to the rooms. The others followed closely behind.

After knocking, Evan opened the door. "Yeah?" He stood in the doorway with a towel wrapped around his waist. His hair was wet.

"Can we talk?" Jamil asked. He glanced at his friends to see if they were wondering the same thing. Why was Evan taking a shower in the middle of the day?

Evan waved them in as he disappeared back into the bathroom. "Let me get dressed. I'll be right out."

As the crew entered the room, Nat quietly started checking it out. She opened the closet door just enough to see inside. She noticed a pile of muddy shorts and T-shirt behind the suitcase, like someone had hastily tried to hide them. She motioned to the others. The crew spread out. Kevin stood by the curtains. Wall sat at the table beside the bed. Nat moved back to the main door. Jamil leaned against the dresser. He slid open the top drawer on a whim. Inside was a large envelope addressed to Splash Boards.

"Hey, guys!" Jamil said as he pulled out the envelope. "I think we've just found the thief and have the evidence to prove it." He slid a large, folded blue sheet of paper out and opened it. On it, black lines showed a wakeboard from several different angles. Measurements and descriptions covered the paper.

"The plans?" Kevin asked excitedly. "Our deception worked!"

Just then, Evan came out of the bathroom dressed.

"Uh-oh." He paused when he saw Jamil reading the blueprints. He turned to run, but Nat was already positioned in front of the door.

"Not this way," she said. She reached behind her and locked the door.

Kevin and Wall stood in front of the window.

Evan slumped onto the bed. "Busted. This day couldn't get any worse."

"Why is that?" Jamil asked.

Evan gave them a wry smile. "I guess you've figured out by now that I'm the one who started the avalanche."

They nodded.

Evan glanced at Jamil's bandaged shin. "I just wanted to give you a scare. I didn't mean for anyone to get hurt."

"You might as well spill it," Nat prodded Evan. "It's all going to come out anyway."

Evan nodded and looked down at his hands. "I stole the plans. I was sick of working for my uncle. This was my chance to score big and finally get away from him."

"Who's your uncle?" Jamil asked shocked.

"Dave Resnick. For the last five years I've been his lackey and I am totally sick of it. He gave me a spare key to his room so I could get Wake Ever stuff for him. That's when I realized I could steal the plans and sell them. I could definitely get some nice change. Then I would be able to spend a couple of years riding full-time. When I heard Splash Boards was making a run at Kyle, I figured they were looking to lay out some major dough." He shrugged. "So I thought I'd sell the plans to them." He paused.

"Then when you heard the announcement at lunch?" Jamil prodded.

"Yeah. I heard Yardley say the plans were no good, but by then I'd already quit Wake Ever and totally dissed the place. After lunch I tried to get my job back, but Uncle Dave just blew his stack. He said he was glad to get rid of me." He looked up at the crew and grimmaced. "When I saw you guys standing behind Yardley during his announcement, I knew you were somehow behind it all." He sunk onto the bed and stared at the floor. "That really sent me over. I had to get back at you guys somehow. So when I saw you leave on the bikes, I figured I'd follow you and see what happened."

Jamil lifted his wounded leg. "If it makes you feel any better, I was almost history."

Evan shook his head. "Of course not. I just went crazy."

"Well, now your day is going to get even worse," Nat said.

"I know," Evan sighed.

"No. You don't. These plans were the right plans," Jamil said as he held up the blueprints. "We got Yardley to lie so that we could trap you."

Evan gulped. "You little jerks! Why, I oughtta—"

"Don't even think about it," Nat stepped forward, glaring down at Evan, her hands on her hips. Wall, Kevin, and Jamil stood behind her.

Knowing he was licked, Evan backed down.

11

A wave of applause erupted into the dining room. Joe Yardley was standing at the front of the room ready to announce the winners of the mystery weekend.

He held up a stack of cards with the guests' solutions written on them. "Our blue ribbon panel of investigators have finally made their decisions." Yardley glanced at the crew and smiled. They had spent dinner reading over the solutions and picking the winners in several categories.

Scattered applause interupted Yardley for a moment.

"The winner of category for weirdest solution is Mike Trevant," Yardley read out loud. "His solution reads, ' I'm guilty. I've always been guilty. It's all my fault. Anything that goes wrong can be traced to me, so forget about everyone else.'"

The room broke into laughter. Mr. Trevant stood and bowed dramatically.

"For that imaginative solution," Yardley continued,

"you've won a pair of wakeboarding gloves."

More applause. Yardley then named the third, second, and first runners-up.

"Now for the grand prize, selected at random from all the winning solutions." Yardley shuffled his cards for a second. "And the winner is Nancy Drood." It was the blond woman who had found the second shoe.

Nancy Drood jumped up, screaming like a contestant in a game show.

Yardley picked up a pair of handcuffs from the table. "Would you do the honors, Ms. Drood?"

Ms. Drood took the handcuffs, walked across the room to Lars, and put them on his wrists. There was a standing ovation as she led Lars back to the front of the room.

Yardley announced her prize—a Kyle Rodriguez signature wakeboard with custom fitted highwraps. Then he held his hand up to quiet the audience one more time. "Now I have one more prize to hand out tonight. And it's for the best detectives in the Rockies!"

Jamil, Nat, Wall, and Kevin looked at each other in confusion. They hadn't voted on this category.

"I'd like to congratulate Jamil, Nat, Wall, and Kevin for solving the real mystery this weekend—the theft of Wake Ever's plans," Yardley explained.

The crew stood and joined Yardley at the front of the room. Mr. Smith leaped up and applauded like a maniac.

"And for their outstanding detective work, Wake Ever is giving each of them their very own wakeboard."

"Oh my gosh!" screamed Jamil.

"All right!" cried Nat as she jumped up and down with excitement.

"Excellent," Kevin added as his head bobbed up and down.

"Solid!" Wall grinned from ear to ear.

Resnick carried the boards into the room and handed one to each of the crew. After the applause died down, the crew returned to their seats.

"I've already arranged with Bob for us to stay a couple of extra days so you guys can stress-test your new boards," Mr. Smith said.

"You knew?" Jamil said, surprised.

Mr. Smith nodded. "Joe told me just before supper. I immediately talked to Bob and he was all for it. In fact, he's so grateful that you're welcome to come anytime to Lake Potow and ride."

"I'm down with that," Wall cracked.

Just then Bob came over to the table. "I want to thank you guys. You saved my business. I don't know how to thank you."

"One thing," Kevin replied. "Why didn't you want the police to be called in?"

Bob flushed. "I didn't want the publicity. I thought maybe April would pull us from next year's schedule if we didn't handle it ourselves."

"But how were you going to handle it?" Jamil asked.

"Like I said this morning," Bob explained, "The cleaning staff did go through the rooms." Bob shrugged.

"Unfortunately, they didn't find anything." He looked at the crew. "So I'm so glad you did."

"Thanks for the extra days' vacation," Wall said.

"My pleasure," responded Bob.

At that moment, Dave Resnick came over to the table. "I just want to thank you. I appreciate you returning the plans."

"I'm sorry about your nephew," Jamil replied.

"I'm not as surprised as you might think. In fact, now that I have the plans back I'm kind of relieved he's no longer working for me," Resnick explained. "He was a real pain."

"Is he gone?" Nat asked.

Resnick nodded.

"He took off right after you guys got through with him," Bob said. "I saw him leave in a cloud of dust."

The next afternoon after all the guests had left, the crew and Mr. Smith were down at the dock ready to ride. They piled into the motorboat with their boards and Mr. Smith pulled the boat away from the dock.

"Who's first?" Mr. Smith asked.

"Me!" they all shouted at once.

"I think I should be first," Jamil said confidently. "I'll show all you beginners how to do it."

Nat leaned back in her seat and pulled her hat over her eyes. "Knock me out, Mr. Expert."

Jamil hopped into the water. Kevin slid his board down to him and then tossed him the rope. In no time

Jamil was set to go. He gave his dad the thumbs-up. His dad gunned it.

Jamil popped up fast. His arms and legs were tucked the way they were supposed to be. He took his time standing, but then the handle slipped from his hands. It was like his hands had suddenly turned to catcher's mitts again.

Jamil groaned in disgust. As the boat circled around, his friends razzed him heavily. Jamil bit his lip and grabbed the rope again.

This time he didn't even get out of the water before he wiped out. For some reason he couldn't bring his board out of the water that time. He felt like he was all elbows.

"Way to go, pro!" Kevin yelled and clapped.

Jamil smiled like he was taking the joke well, but he wasn't. He was going to try one more time and then give up. He tried to visualize what he needed to do. Then he gave his dad a thumbs-up. Mr. Smith gunned it.

Jamil popped up and suddenly felt relaxed. His body was doing what it was supposed to. He shot across a wake and rode wide for a moment. Just then the echo of his dad's voice creeped into his mind. It said, "Be persistent in good actions."

Even though Jamil still had no clue what his dad meant, in the back of his mind he knew it had something to do with not giving up.

He cut a progressive edge and did a two-wake 180 into the glorious afternoon.

Glossary

Backside: The heelside edge of a board.

Backside 360: Rider approaches regular, performs a 360-degree rotation while crossing both wakes and lands in the forward position on the opposite side of the second wake.

Biff: crash.

Dock Start: The rider starts standing or sitting on the dock and the boat pulls him out.

Double-up: A term that describes a type of wake that is created when the boat does a wide turn and crosses over the old wake. The rider cuts on the inside of the turn and when the wakes cross, he cuts back and hits the wakes at the point where they come together. The wakes crossing together form a "double up," virtually three times the size of a normal wake.

Fakie: Riding the board backward.

Half-Cab: Rider approaches fakie, performs a 180-degree rotation while crossing both wakes in the air and lands in a forward position on the opposite side of the second wake.

Krypt: A raley except the rider lands fakie.

Progressive: A deeply cut edge, usually done on the heelside of the board.

Raley: The rider hits the wake and allows his board and body to swing up over his head while he crosses the wake. Rider then swings the board and body down and lands on the opposite side of the wake.

Revert: Fakie.

Roll: A rider approaches the wake and rolls the board around and over his head.

Scarecrow: A front roll to revert in which the rider lands fakie.

Speedball: A double front flip.

Surface 360: The rider spins his board 360 degrees while keeping it on the surface of the water.

Tantrum: A back flip over the wake.

Two-wake 180: Rider approaches regular, performs a 180-degree rotation while crossing both wakes in the air and lands fakie on the opposite side of the second wake.

Whirlybird: A twist on a tantrum whereupon the rider adds a 360 to the backflip.

Check out more rad lingo on ESPN's Xgames website: http://ESPN.SportsZone.com